the historical strips
of jack jackson

FANTAGRAPHICS BOOKS

7563 Lake City Way N.E.
Seattle, WA

Edited and art directed by Mark Thompson
Design by Pat Moriarity & Mark Thompson
Cover colored by Jim Woodring
Cover color separations by Rayson Films
Special thanks to Jeremy Eaton & Scott Semans

First Fantagraphics Books edition: May, 1995
1 3 5 7 9 10 8 6 4 2

ISBN: 1-56097-171-1

Printed in Canada

God's Bosom

and other stories

the historical strips
of jack jackson

FANTAGRAPHICS BOOKS

Seattle, WA

the historical strips of jack jackson

JAXON'S Illustrated TALES

No. 1

$1.25

SPECIAL ISSUE: SPANISH TEXAS

introduction

This book of historical strips is roughly divided into two parts, past and present.

Part One kicks off with my CAMINO REAL COMICS, a strip done recently for the Texas Highway Department and intended as a booklet which they would distribute free to the public school system for use in the junior-high Texas history course. Its purpose was to commemorate the 300th anniversary of the first road blazed across Texas (1691-1991), often called the "Old San Antonio Road," and to show how the present road system developed from this humble Spanish beginning. Having been exposed to a comic-book treatment of Texas history in my own youth, it had always been a dream of mine to do something along these lines for today's kiddos. Alas, the THD did not follow through on the project, much to my dismay. The story is presented here as an example of how the medium can be used to educate younger readers about the history of their region while entertaining them as well.

Following this "tame" strip are several examples of my more outrageous treatments of the Spanish colonial period. The first, GOD'S BOSOM, is based on an actual event: a shipwreck that took place off the Texas coast in 1554. The story is presented with very little deviation from the known facts — except for how the ordeal unhinged Father Mena's mind, an undocumented twist but one which likely occurred. Next is a three-part (fictional) series, comprising THE GOOD LIFE, THE SAVAGE WITHIN and POSSUM ON A STICK, concerning life at the Texas missions and the difficulties the padres faced as they attempted to convert their Indian charges from a life of savagery overnight. Through the example of one promising neophyte, Yoyo Pintado, we see how their efforts sometimes failed. One of the characters in this series is Diego Gortari, a prototypical Spanish scout from my yarn *The Secret of San Saba*. The latter, in turn, is an extract from a novel I've written, which I don't expect to see published during my lifetime. Too controversial.

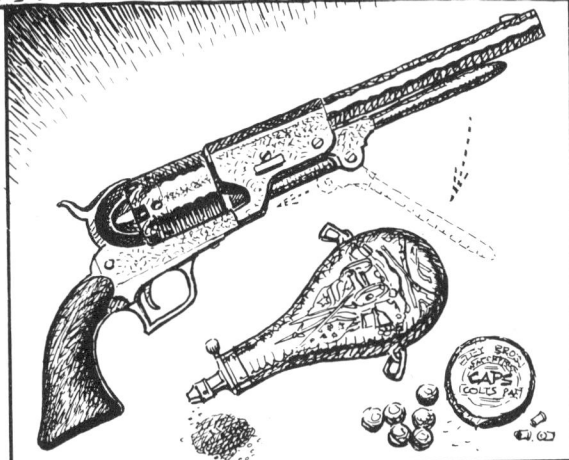

What he came up with was an awesome weapon — six shots instead of five, .44 instead of .36 caliber, a lever which permitted reloading without tearing down the gun, a trigger guard, and a hefty weight of 4½ pounds.

Not to neglect the later Anglo period, two strips are included. THE COLT REVOLVER AND THE TEXAS RANGERS (unpublished) is a humorous look at the impact that Colt's invention had on frontier warfare. It is carefully researched, as is NITS MAKE LICE — one of my attempts to dispense with the romantic bullshit about the Winning of the West. Although this episode took place outside of Texas, other equally horrendous Indian slaughters can be documented on Texas soil and, indeed, throughout the American West. It was a matter of degree, not substance, this United States policy of genocide.

Somewhat less depressing is Part Two, which features examples of my satirical commentary on contemporary subjects. RIP OFF PRESS: THE GOLDEN ERA looks at the early years of this underground publishing house and the characters involved (including myself). After my West Coast burnout and return to Texas, I tried my hand at lampooning the cultural craziness in Austin, long the center of artistic ferment in the state. Most of these strips appeared in a local "alternative" newspaper, *The Austin Sun*, but were met with no great enthusiasm. People who fancy themselves on the cutting edge of a cultural phenomenon find it difficult to laugh at themselves. This was true of the hippie scene in San Francisco and no less true of the cosmic cowboy phase in Austin. In fact, it was worse here because Texas had always been a cultural wasteland, and the natives saw the music scene as their best shot at long-overdue national recognition. The last thing they wanted was some wise-ass taking cheap shots and making fun of the vibrant homegrown scene-in-progress.

About this time began the Yankee invasion of Texas, land speculation by outsiders in the

Sun Belt zone, and other obnoxious happenings which (mercifully) culminated in the S&L scandals and Land Bust of the '80s. The rapid changes in what had always been a mellow, laid-back Texan lifestyle prompted me to do several jaundiced strips about this period. I wrote others, even more resentful and bitter, but never drew them as there was no point in doing so. Hell, even my old radical friends were cashing in on the land bonanza and the rising real estate prices! Anyway, these blasts would have never seen publication, as Texans were assiduously courting the influx of foreigners and intent on bowing down to the Almighty Dollar. Even as I write, this "Development" cycle is repeating itself after lying dormant for a few years after the Bust. Probably by the end of the century, Texas will be as fucked-up as the rest of the country and will retain little of its original flavor.

Like some ethnic or religious groups, Texans have always considered themselves special and have ferociously clung to their traditions. I confess to being guilty of this cultural nationalism, but I also see Texas as a microcosmic reflection of the human experience on the planet itself. Thus my preoccupation with history and how little human nature has changed through the loop of time. We think we're advancing and getting better, but, like Yoyo Pintado, events crash down on us every once in a while and we come face-to-face with the savage within.

Is there any salvation? Probably not, but it helps to have a sense of humor about events past, present and future. If people took themselves less seriously, many of the world's ills

would appear less dire and some of them would vanish overnight. That won't happen, of course, so we may as well laugh about it instead of cry, right? Life zooms by too fast to sit around moping; live it with zest and move on to the next stage. If we were sup-

posed to know what it was all about, we'd have figured it out by now. Since we haven't we might as well have a chuckle about our predicament while we still can.

My last strip, about Oat Willie's mid-life crisis, pretty much sums up my present attitude about the world's problems and what we as individuals can do to solve them: not much, but at least we can make our own choices (to a certain degree) in the way we live. Like God Nose says, we can "do our part" and that's about it. We mortals are ill-equiped to carry the weight of the world on our shoulders, and we let life pass us by in the process.

Here today, gone tomorrow, will always be one of my favorite gems of wisdom, along with "he never knew what hit him." Individually, our dip in the gene pool is of brief duration, but it is fascinating to look at how our predecessors tested the waters and to wonder how future generations will fare in the ol' swimming hole of life. Hopefully, it will be with a grin of delight, or at least a sardonic smile in acknowledgment that this is too good to last. The sensible thing, it seems to me, is to enjoy it while it does.

—JACK JACKSON

Part 1.

~Old Tejas~

CaminoReal COMICS

THE KING'S HIGHWAY ACROSS TEXAS

LONG BEFORE ANY EUROPEANS ARRIVED, TEXAS WAS CRISS-CROSSED BY INDIAN TRAILS.
THE INDIANS TRAVELED THEM TO HUNT, GATHER, AND TRADE WITH NEIGHBORING TRIBES.

AT FAVORITE CAMPSITES ALONG THESE PATHS, THE INDIANS LEFT REMINDERS THAT THEY WERE HERE BEFORE US.

THE ROADS WEREN'T VERY FANCY, BUT KEEP IN MIND THAT THERE WEREN'T A LOT OF TOURISTS IN THOSE DAYS EITHER.

FOR 200 YEARS AFTER COLUMBUS "DISCOVERED" AMERICA THE INDIANS OF TEXAS WERE LEFT PRETTY MUCH TO THEMSELVES.

ALL THIS CHANGED IN 1684, WHEN THE FRENCH "SUN KING," LOUIS XIV, DECIDED TO ESTABLISH A COLONY ON THE LOWER MISSISSIPPI RIVER.

THE BRAINS BEHIND THE SCHEME WAS SIEUR DE LA SALLE, WHO HAD FLOATED ALL THE WAY DOWNRIVER FROM CANADA TWO YEARS EARLIER.

IT'S NOT FAIR FOR SPAIN TO HOG ALL THE GOLD AND SILVER IN AMERICA.

NOT FAIR AT ALL, YOUR MAJESTY!

SEE? FROM THE RIVER'S MOUTH IT'S ONLY A SHORT TRIP TO THE RICH SPANISH MINES.

MY, THAT IS CLOSE!

LA SALLE THOUGHT THAT THE MISSISSIPPI ENTERED THE GULF RIGHT NEXT TO THE RIO GRANDE.

IS THIS THE PLACE?

DEFINITELY — I'D RECOGNIZE IT ANYWHERE.

SO HE WENT ASHORE AT MATAGORDA BAY, FIGURING IT WAS THE MISSISSIPPI DELTA, AND HIS SHIPS SAILED BACK TO FRANCE.

BUILD A STOCKADE AND SOME CABINS OVER THERE WHILE I GO FIND THE RIVER.

IT DIDN'T TAKE LA SALLE LONG TO REALIZE THAT HE WAS LOST.

THERE IT IS!

NO! NO! IT'S BIGGER THAN THAT, MUCH BIGGER!

WHILE LA SALLE LOOKED FOR THE MIGHTY MISSISSIPPI, SO HE COULD REACH CANADA, AND GET HELP, HIS COLONY SUFFERED FROM SICKNESS AND STARVATION.

HMM... THIS ROAD ISN'T ON THE MAP.

ON ONE OF THESE EXPLORATIONS, LA SALLE WAS KILLED NEAR THE TRINITY BY SOME OF HIS MEN.

NOW WE'RE IN A REAL MESS!

NO WORSE OFF THAN BEFORE.

THE INDIANS FINISHED OFF WHAT WAS LEFT OF HIS PITIFUL COLONY, BUT A FEW PEOPLE MANAGED TO SURVIVE.

BOY, GO FETCH SOME FIREWOOD.

YESSUM.

WORD OF LA SALLE'S DARING VENTURE SOON REACHED OFFICIALS IN NEW SPAIN, AS MEXICO WAS CALLED IN THOSE DAYS.

THE NERVE OF THOSE FRENCHMEN, TRYING TO STEAL OUR LAND.

LET'S KICK 'EM OUT!

GUIDES WERE USED ON THE FIRST SPANISH ATTEMPTS TO LOCATE THE FRENCH INTRUDERS IN THE UNCHARTED WILDERNESS.

DON'T WORRY. I'VE BEEN TO TH' COAST A BUNCH OF TIMES GOIN' DOWN THIS WAY.

ARE WE LOST, OR WHAT?

ON HIS FOURTH EXPEDITION, IN 1689, GENERAL ALONSO DE LEÓN FINALLY FOUND THE FRENCH FORT.

DE LEÓN CAME BACK A YEAR LATER, TO BURN WHAT WAS LEFT OF THE RUINS. THEN HE WENT FURTHER NORTH, TO THE NECHES RIVER, AND ESTABLISHED A MISSION FOR THE TEJAS INDIANS.

IN 1691, DOMINGO TERÁN, THE FIRST GOVERNOR OF TEXAS, STRUCK OUT AGAIN FROM COAHUILA. HE WANTED TO BUILD MORE MISSIONS IN EAST TEXAS.

TERÁN'S EXPEDITION FORGED THE ROUTE ACROSS TEXAS KNOWN TO US EVER SINCE AS EL CAMINO REAL, THE KING'S HIGHWAY.

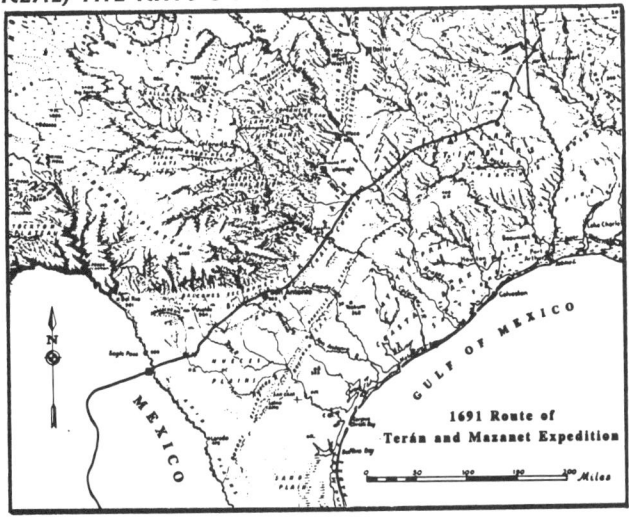

ALTHOUGH TERÁN'S ROAD WAS THE MOST POPULAR ROUTE TO NACOGDOCHES FOR MANY YEARS, LATER TRIPS OFTEN HAD TO TAKE DETOURS.

SOMETIMES THE PROBLEM WAS JUST THE OPPOSITE.

THUS, OVER THE YEARS THE KING'S HIGHWAY BECAME MORE OF A CORRIDOR, A NETWORK OF TRAILS GOING IN THE SAME DIRECTION, THAN A SINGLE ROAD.

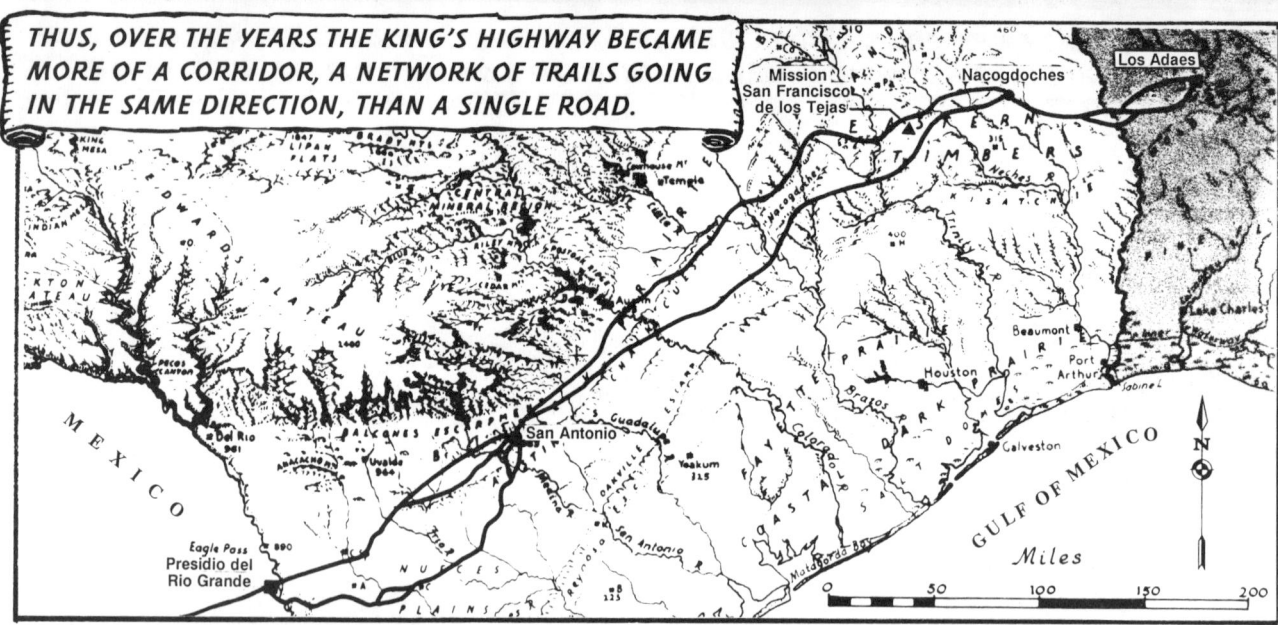

WHEN THE EAST TEXAS MISSIONS WERE CLOSED IN 1693, THE KING'S HIGHWAY GREW UP WITH WEEDS AND STAYED THAT WAY FOR TWENTY YEARS.

THEN, IN 1714, A YOUNG FRENCHMAN NAMED SAINT-DENIS CAME DOWN THE TRAIL FROM LOUISIANA TO TRADE WITH THE SPANIARDS.

THIS TIME WE'LL LEAVE NOT ONLY PRIESTS BUT SOLDIERS TOO.

SAN ANTONIO WAS FOUNDED IN 1718 AS A WAY-STATION ON THE ROAD BACK TO NACOGDOCHES.

THIS'LL BE A BIG CITY SOMEDAY.

YOU THINK SO?

THREE YEARS LATER A NEW GOVERNOR, THE MARQUÉS DE AGUAYO, EXTENDED THE KING'S HIGHWAY ON EASTWARD TO THE LOUISIANA BORDER, WHERE HE BUILT A STRONG FORT.

WE CAN KEEP AN EYE ON THOSE CRAFTY FRENCHMEN FROM HERE.

THIS PRESIDIO AT LOS ADAES (PRESENT ROBELINE, LA.) WAS THE CAPITAL OF TEXAS FOR FIFTY YEARS, AND THE END OF THE LINE FOR PEOPLE TRAVELING UP THE CAMINO REAL FROM MEXICO.

DURING THE 1740s, A MORE SOUTHERN ROUTE WAS OPENED BETWEEN SAN JUAN BAUTISTA AND SAN ANTONIO, CALLED THE "LOWER PRESIDIO ROAD."

YEAH, BUT NOBODY EVER SHOWS UP ..

IF THIS ONE'S ANY BETTER, I'D HATE TO SEE WHAT THE UPPER ROAD IS LIKE!

FROM SAN ANTONIO TO LOS ADAES THE ROAD STAYED THE SAME AND CONTINUED TO BE CALLED "CAMINO DE LOS TEJAS."

IT TOOK A MULE TRAIN ABOUT A MONTH TO TRAVEL BETWEEN THE SETTLEMENTS.

TO GO TO SALTILLO, THE BIG MARKETPLACE IN COAHUILA WHERE TEXAS GOT MOST OF ITS SUPPLIES, TOOK ANOTHER MONTH.

THERE WEREN'T ANY MOTELS OR CAFES ALONG THE WAY EITHER. JUST SOME FREQUENTLY USED PARAJES (ROADSIDE RESTSTOPS OR CAMPSITES).

IF THE APACHES OR COMANCHES WERE ON THE WARPATH, TRAVELERS HAD TO WAIT UNTIL A LARGE MILITARY ESCORT WAS AVAILABLE.

BUT I'M IN A HURRY — I'VE GOT TO LEAVE NOW!

THEN MY ADVICE IS TO PICK OUT A COFFIN FIRST.

A MAIL SERVICE DIDN'T EXIST UNTIL 1779.

JUST THINK — NOW WE'LL GET LETTERS ONCE A MONTH!!

I'LL BELIEVE IT WHEN I SEE IT.

REGLAMENTO de CORREOS

THE 1200-MILE TRIP BETWEEN NACOGDOCHES AND THE SEAT OF GOVERNMENT IN ARISPE, SONORA, WAS A LONG LONELY HAUL FOR POSTMEN.

THERE'S GOTTA BE A BETTER WAY TO MAKE A LIVING.

BEGINNING IN THE MID-1770s THE CAMINO REAL HEADING SOUTH WAS USED AS A CATTLE TRAIL.

GIT ALONG, LITTLE OREJANOS!

AFTER SPAIN DECLARED WAR AGAINST ENGLAND IN 1779, HERDS ALSO WENT UP THE TRAIL TO LOUISIANA.

LOOK OUT OPELOUSAS, HERE WE COME!

THUS, THE SPANISH ARMY THAT FOUGHT THE BRITISH ALONG THE GULF DURING THE AMERICAN REVOLUTION ATE TEXAS BEEF!

THIS TRADE WITH LOUISIANA, WHICH HAD ALWAYS BEEN ILLEGAL, PROVED HARD TO STOP ONCE THE WAR WAS OVER.

IF CAUGHT, SMUGGLERS LOST THEIR CATTLE, HAD TO PAY STEEP FINES, AND WERE PUT TO WORK ON PROJECTS LIKE ROAD REPAIRS.

THE CAMINO REAL AND ITS NETWORK OF ADJOINING ROADS ALSO SERVED AS BOUNDARIES FOR VARIOUS LAND GRANTS.

AT FIRST THE MISSIONS GOT MOST OF THESE GRANTS, AND THEY WERE LARGE — UP TO ELEVEN LEAGUES (OVER 48,000 ACRES).

BUT WHEN THE DEMAND FOR BEEF PICKED UP, PRIVATE CITIZENS ALSO APPLIED FOR LAND TOO.

MY RANCH IS DOWNRIVER, RIGHT NEXT TO THE MISSION'S PASTURE... HEH HEH..

RANCH HOUSES WERE USUALLY BUILT CLOSE TO ROADS, SO THEY MADE CONVENIENT REST STOPS.

STAY AWHILE — IT'S A LONG WAY TO THE NEXT RANCH.

THIS HELPED TRAVELERS, SINCE THERE WEREN'T ANY INNS, AND IT GAVE THE LONELY RANCHERS SOME COMPANY TOO.

SO TELL ME THE LATEST HAPPENINGS IN TH' BIG CITY.

THE CAMINO DE LOS TEJAS, GOING FROM SAN ANTONIO TO NACOGDOCHES, CHANGED JUST BEFORE THE TURN OF THE CENTURY.

IT'S ABOUT TIME!

ABOVE PRESENT-DAY SAN MARCOS IT BRANCHED OFF THE OLD ROUTE. MODERN STATE HIGHWAY 21 FOLLOWS ITS COURSE TO EAST TEXAS.

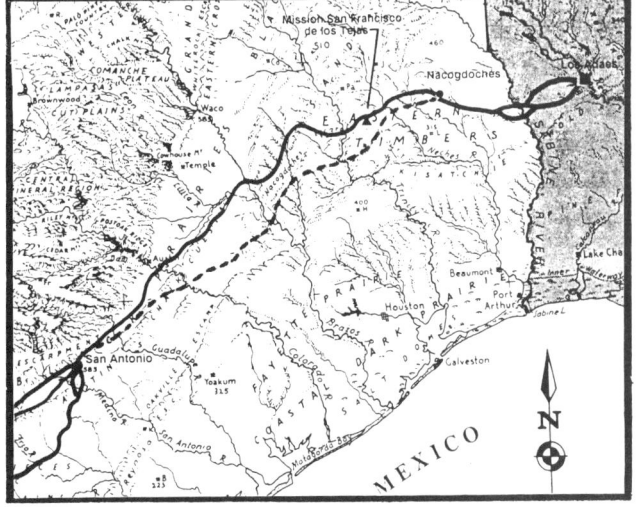

THIS MEANT THAT TRAVELERS TAKING THE NEW ROAD COULD NO LONGER ENJOY THE ICE-COLD SPRINGS AT THE SITE OF MODERN AUSTIN.

I'M GONNA MISS THIS.

THAT'S PROGRESS FOR YOU.

THE NEW ROUTE WAS CALLED THE CAMINO ARRIBA (HIGH ROAD), EVEN THOUGH IT RAN BELOW THE ABANDONED CAMINO DE LOS TEJAS ROUTE.

...RIGHT THOUGH THE THICKEST WOODS IMAGINABLE!

AROUND 1806 GOVERNOR ANTONIO CORDERO ORDERED THE OLD UPPER PRESIDIO ROAD REOPENED. IT BECAME KNOWN AS THE CAMINO PITA.

NOW IF THE GOVERNOR WOULD JUST GET IT PAVED...

DON'T GIVE HIM ANY IDEAS — OUR TAXES ARE HIGH ENUFF ALREADY!

PITA TRAIL, AS IT WAS LATER CALLED, TOOK A DIFFERENT APPROACH TO SAN ANTONIO FROM THE FRIO RIVER ON, MUCH LIKE TERÁN'S ROUTE.

IT'LL TAKE THE INDIANS AWHILE TO FIGURE IT OUT.

BESIDES THE CAMINO REAL CORRIDOR, TEXAS HAD ONLY A FEW OTHER MAIN ROADS AT THE BEGINNING OF THE 19TH CENTURY.

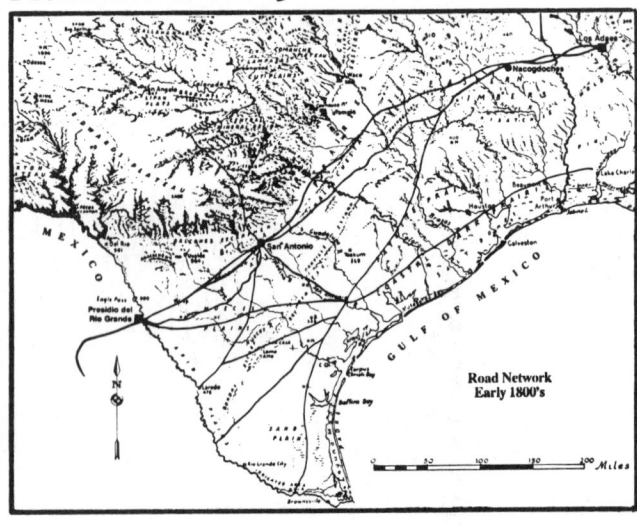

Road Network
Early 1800's

THIS IS UNDERSTANDABLE BECAUSE SPAIN WANTED TO KEEP FOREIGNERS OUT OF TEXAS.

THE FEWER ROADS, THE LESS TRAFFIC WE GOTTA WORRY ABOUT!

STILL, AMERICANS BEGAN TO TRICKLE IN, USING INDIAN TRAILS OR CUTTING NEW ONES THROUGH THE WOODS.

ROADS? WHO NEEDS ROADS?

SOME OF THEM, LIKE PHILIP NOLAN, WERE AFTER WILD HORSES.

HORSES BRING A LOT OF MONEY IN NATCHEZ AND NEW ORLEANS THESE DAYS.

NOLAN'S DEATH IN 1801 DIDN'T DO MUCH TO STEM THE FLOW OF AMERICANS PUSHING WESTWARD.

THAT'S THE END OF THAT!

THAT'S WHAT YOU THINK!

THE LOUISIANA PURCHASE OF 1803 MADE THE SPANIARDS EVEN MORE ANXIOUS ABOUT PROTECTING THEIR EXPOSED TEXAS FRONTIER.

JEFFERSON CLAIMS THAT LOUISIANA GOES ALL THE WAY TO THE RIO GRANDE.

WHAT?! THAT'S OUTRAGEOUS!

WAR ALMOST BROKE OUT BECAUSE SPAIN AND THE UNITED STATES COULDN'T AGREE ON THEIR NEW BOUNDARY LINE.

EVERYTHING BETWEEN THE RED RIVER AND THE SABINE WAS DECLARED A "NEUTRAL GROUND," OR NO-MAN'S-LAND, UNTIL DIPLOMATS COULD SETTLE THE QUESTION. TRAVEL BECAME DANGEROUS.

IN RESPONSE TO THE THREAT TWO NEW SETTLEMENTS WERE FOUNDED ON THE CAMINO REAL — AT THE SAN MARCOS AND TRINITY RIVER CROSSINGS. IT WAS TOO LITTLE, TOO LATE.

THE COMANCHES RAN THE SETTLERS OUT OF SAN MARCOS DE NEVE, AND TRINIDAD DE SALCEDO NEVER AMOUNTED TO MUCH.

SEVERAL YEARS LATER AN ARMY OF FILIBUSTERS USED THE CAMINO REAL TO RIDE INTO NACOGDOCHES.

GUTIÉRREZ AND MAGEE, THE EXPEDITION'S LEADERS, DECLARED TEXAS A REPUBLIC WHEN THEY REACHED THE DESERTED TRINITY OUTPOST.

NEXT THEY TOOK LA BAHÍA (GOLIAD) AND HEADED FOR OLD SAN ANTONIO.

BUT A SPANISH ARMY UNDER GENERAL JOACHIN DE ARREDONDO QUICKLY MARCHED UP FROM LAREDO.

ONE OF ARREDONDO'S OFFICERS, COLONEL IGNACIO ELIZONDO, CHASED THE SURVIVORS UP THE CAMINO REAL TO THE TRINITY RIVER.

AFTER ARREDONDO'S PURGE, TEXAS WAS A WASTELAND FOR YEARS.

IN 1820 AN AMERICAN NAMED MOSES AUSTIN RODE DOWN THE KING'S HIGHWAY, OR OLD SAN ANTONIO, WITH HOPES OF SETTLING THREE HUNDRED FAMILIES IN TEXAS.

WHEN MOSES DIED, THE EMPRESARIO CONTRACT HE HAD OBTAINED FROM MEXICO PASSED TO HIS SON, STEPHEN.

THE OLD SAN ANTONIO ROAD SERVED AS A BOUNDARY LINE FOR SOME OF THE EMPRESARIO GRANTS JUST AS VARIOUS CAMINOS HAD FOR EARLIER LAND GRANTS.

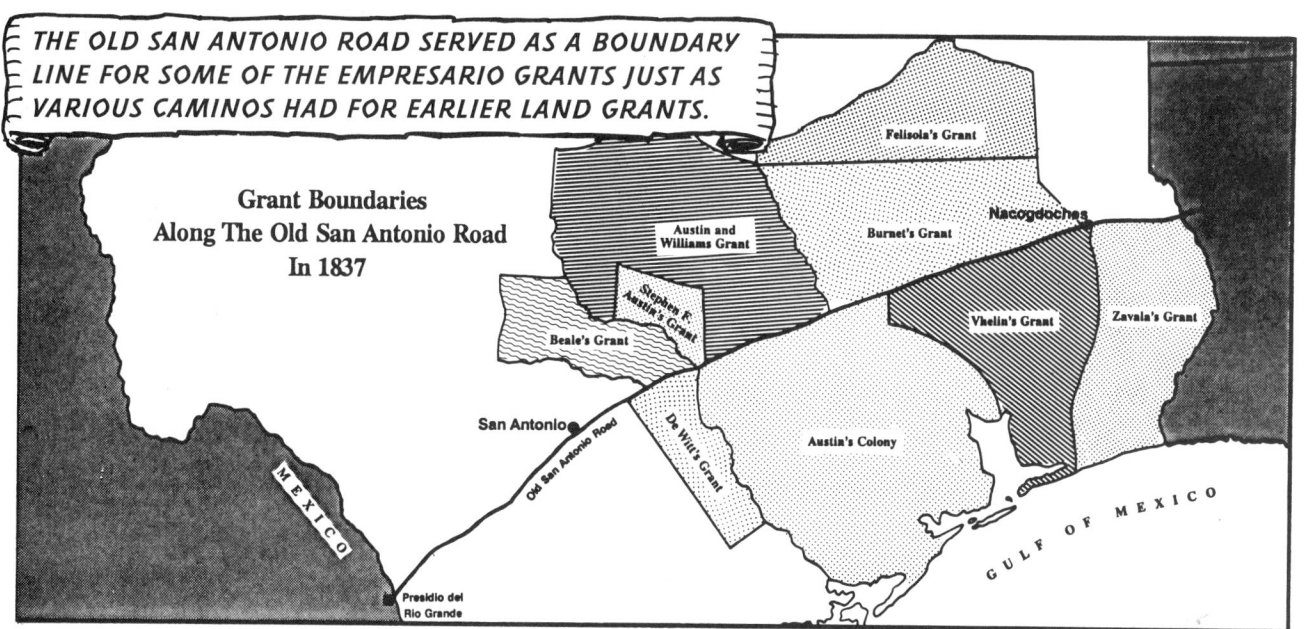

Grant Boundaries
Along The Old San Antonio Road
In 1837

Felisola's Grant

Austin and Williams Grant

Burnet's Grant

Nacogdoches

Stephen F. Austin's Grant

Vhelin's Grant

Zavala's Grant

Beale's Grant

De Witt's Grant

San Antonio

Old San Antonio Road

Austin's Colony

MEXICO

GULF OF MEXICO

Presidio del Rio Grande

AS ANGLO COLONISTS MOVED INTO TEXAS DURING THE 1820s, NEW TOWNS SPRANG UP AND THE NETWORK OF ROADS RAPIDLY EXPANDED.

WHAT'S THE BEST ROUTE TO SAN ANTONE, FRIEND?

TAKE TH' SAN FELIPE THRU' GONZALES — IT'S NEW!

EMPRESARIOS WERE RESPONSIBLE FOR MAINTAINING THE NEW ROADS IN THEIR GRANTS.

WE NEED WAGON ROADS, NOT JUST MULE TRAILS.

PLAT MAPS DRAWN BY SURVEYORS USUALLY SHOWED THE OLD SPANISH ROADS AND RIVER CROSSINGS.

WHAT CAUSED THESE DEEP RUTS, JOSÉ?

MANY PACK TRAINS, SEÑOR.

THE CAMINO ARRIBA WAS STILL TRAVELED BUT THE OLDER TEJAS TRAIL SAW LESS AND LESS USE AS OTHER ROADS CAME INTO BEING.

DURING THE TEXAS REVOLUTION, A MAJOR BATTLE TOOK PLACE AT AN OLD MISSION THAT SAT SQUARELY ON THE CAMINO REAL.

THE EXPANDED ROAD SYSTEM WAS CRITICAL TO TROOP MOVEMENTS ON BOTH SIDES.

AFTER INDEPENDENCE PEOPLE POURED INTO TEXAS FROM THE UNITED STATES OVER SUCH UPPER ROUTES AS TRAMMELL'S TRACE.

PORTS WERE OPENED AND MORE NEW ROADS LINKED THE INTERIOR TO THESE BUSTLING TRADE CENTERS ALONG THE GULF COAST.

IN 1839 PRESIDENT MIRABEAU LAMAR MOVED THE CAPITAL FROM HOUSTON TO A REMOTE SPOT WHERE THE CAMINO DE LOS TEJAS CROSSED THE COLORADO RIVER.

WE'LL CALL IT "AUSTIN."

KINDA OFF TH' BEATEN PATH, ISN'T IT?

DURING THE REPUBLIC SEVERAL MEXICAN RAIDS WERE LAUNCHED AGAINST TEXAS BUT NONE GOT PAST SAN ANTONIO.

I HEREBY DECLARE YOU TO BE CITIZENS OF MEXICO — AGAIN!

ONE OF THESE FORAYS, LED BY GENERAL ADRIAN WOLL, TOOK A ROUTE ABOVE THE OLD UPPER PRESIDIO ROAD. "WOLL'S ROAD" IS NOW U.S. HIGHWAY 90 BETWEEN UVALDE AND SAN ANTONIO.

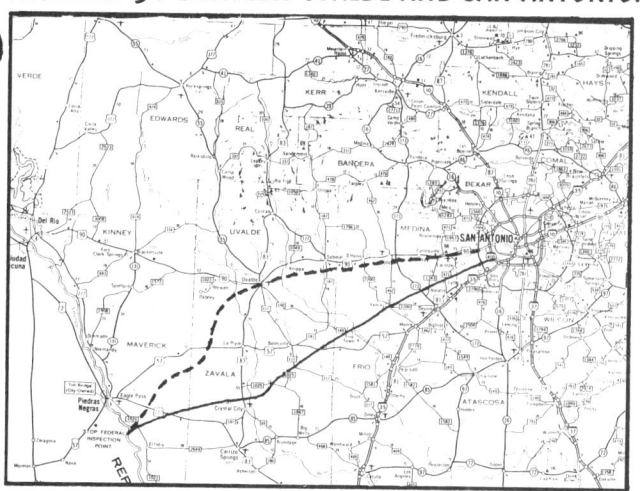

WHEN THE MEXICAN WAR BROKE OUT IN 1846, BRIGADIER GENERAL JOHN E. WOOL INVADED MEXICO VIA WOLL'S ROAD.

IF IT WAS GOOD ENUFF FOR WOLL, THEN IT'S GOOD ENUFF FOR WOOL!

SOME SECTIONS OF THE KING'S HIGHWAY WERE ALMOST LOST TO MEMORY.

LEMME SEE NOW, I THINK IT CAME THRU OVER THERE — OR DID IT?

FINALLY, IN 1911 MRS. CLAUDIA NORVELL, A MEMBER OF THE DAUGHTERS OF THE AMERICAN REVOLUTION, DECIDED THAT THE OLD SAN ANTONIO ROAD DESERVED SOME ATTENTION.

IT'S OLDER THAN THE SANTA FE TRAIL, THAT'S FOR SURE!

SHE WORKED WITH A CIVIL ENGINEER, V.N. ZIVLEY, WHO DID A CAREFUL SURVEY OF THE SPANISH CAMINO REAL.

HERE IT HEADS ACROSS THAT WAY.

PINK GRANITE MARKERS WERE PLACED EVERY 5 MILES ALONG THE ROUTE FROM THE SABINE TO THE RIO GRANDE.

KING'S HIGHWAY
CAMINO REAL
OLD SAN ANTONIO ROAD
MARKED BY THE
DAUGHTERS OF THE
AMERICAN REVOLUTION
AND THE STATE OF TEXAS
A.D. 1918

AFTER THE CREATION OF THE STATE HIGHWAY DEPARTMENT IN 1917, SOME PEOPLE URGED THAT A MODERN HIGHWAY BE BUILT FOLLOWING ZIVLEY'S SURVEY.

IT WOULD PRESERVE AN IMPORTANT PART OF OUR HERITAGE.

IT NEVER HAPPENED, BUT A NUMBER OF DIFFERENT HIGHWAYS STILL RUN NEAR PORTIONS OF THE ANCIENT TRAIL. THIS YEAR, 1991, MARKS THE 300TH ANNIVERSARY OF THE FIRST ROAD ACROSS TEXAS, EL CAMINO REAL, LATER KNOWN AS THE OLD SAN ANTONIO ROAD.

JAXON·91

END

DAWN BREAKS OVER THE ANCIENT CITY OF CUZCO, ITS GREAT CATHEDRAL LOOMING ABOVE MASSIVE STONES OF THE DEMOLISHED INCA SUN TEMPLE.

WITHIN, AN OLD FRIAR SITS ALONE IN HIS CELL, OBLIVIOUS TO THE NEW DAY.

AHH... GOOD MORNING FRAY MARCOS. UP EARLY I SEE...

SMELL THAT AIR, EH? LISTEN TO THE BIRDS SINGING OUTSIDE. THE WORLD IS COMING ALIVE!

YESSS... I HEAR... IT...

THEN LAY ASIDE YOUR WORK AND JOIN US. THE INDIANS ARE COMING TODAY TO DANCE...

NO...NO... IT'S SO PEACEFUL NOW. I... I THINK I'LL STAY... HERE, SAFE IN GOD'S...GOD'S...

© jaxon 1983

God's Bosom

MEMORIES CLAIM FRAY MARCOS AND TAKE HIM BACK, AS THEY ALWAYS DO, TO THE YEAR 1554. THE ANNUAL TREASURE FLOTA FINDS ITSELF LASHED BY GALE WINDS, CAST BACK UPON THE BLEAK TEXAS SHORELINE — STILL TERRA INCOGNITA TO HAPLESS SPANISH MARINERS.

ADMIRAL, WE'VE HIT A SANDBAR! THE SHIP IS BREAKING UP!!

THEN WE MUST CAST OURSELVES UP- ON GOD'S BOSOM — THE SEA!

BUT THE RAGING SEA OFFERS NO PROTECTION FOR MANY OF ESPÍRITU SANTO'S PASSENGERS.

UNLESS ONE CONSIDERS THE WATERY DEPTHS A SHELTER...AND THE COLD FINGERS OF DEATH A WELCOME EMBRACE.

LESS THAN A THIRD OF THE DAZED, DISHEVELED VOYAGERS SURVIVE TO REACH SHORE. AMONG THEM IS FRAY MARCOS DE MENA, A YOUNG DOMINICAN FRIAR BOUND FOR THE EASY LIFE BACK IN SPAIN.

IGNORING BOXES AND CASKS OF PROVISIONS THAT WASH ASHORE THEY SET OUT DOWN THE COASTLINE EMPTY HANDED, BELIEVING TAMPICO TO BE ONLY THREE DAYS' JOURNEY.

AFTER WALKING SIX DAYS HUNGER GNAWS AT THEIR VITALS, A HUNGER THAT NOT EVEN FEAR CAN CONQUER.

SUCH AS FEAR OF THE SAVAGE KARANKAWAS!

ABANDONING HIS PRIZE, PEDRO MENDEZ FLEES.

INDIANS, IN-DIANS! OVER THERE!!

THE NEWS SPREADS CONSTERNATION.

INDIANS.

DID THEY **ATTACK** YOU?

HOW MANY?

WHAT SHALL WE DO??

I WO SEE IT!

A FEW, LIKE FRAY MARCOS, HAVE READ CABEZA DE VACA'S RECENT BOOK OF HIS WANDERINGS AND MANY TRIBULATIONS IN THIS DESOLATE LAND.

THEY ARE A BRUTISH AND FEROCIOUS PEOPLE WHO WILL ENSLAVE US. PRAY TO GOD!!

MERCIFULLY, THESE CASTAWAYS ARE IGNORANT OF A GRIM CUSTOM THE KARANKAWAS HAVE ADOPTED SINCE THEIR MEETING WITH DE VACA'S DESTITUTE PARTY — CANNIBALISM!

NO PANIC! LET US FIRST DISCOVER THEIR INTENTIONS.

NONETHELESS, WITH MIXED EMOTIONS THEY AWAIT THE COMING OF THE PAGANS.

LOOK! THERE THEY ARE!!!

KEEP CALM... SHOW NO FEAR.

CHRIST IS OUR SHIELD.

AIEEE!

HOLY MARY, MOTHER OF GOD...

DESPITE THEIR FORMIDABLE APPEARANCE THE INDIANS SEEM TO BE FRIENDLY. THEY BRING VENISON, FISH AND THE FIRE TO COOK IT WITH.

FOOD!

FOOD!

WHILE THE VICTUALS ARE ROASTING, THE GUILEFUL CANNIBALS CONTINUE PROTESTATIONS OF FRIENDSHIP, URGING THE SPANISH TO RELAX AND EAT.

AS THE AROMA OF COOKING MEAT TANTALIZES THE FAMISHED THRONG, ONLY THE FLEET'S CAPTAIN GENERAL CAUTIONS VIGILANCE.

THEY BRING TOO MUCH FOOD TO BE ENEMIES, BUT TOO MANY WEAPONS TO BE FRIENDS...

BE READY!

BUT HIS ADMONITIONS ARE SOON FORGOTTEN WHEN THE FEASTING BEGINS.

...WHICH IS WHAT THE INDIANS HAVE BEEN WAITING FOR!

AIIEEEEEEE!

ARMED WITH NOTHING BUT A FEW SWORDS AND TWO CROSSBOWS, THE SPANIARDS REPEL THEIR ATTACK...

... AND FLEE DOWN THE BEACH, EMPTY STOMACHS STILL GROWLING.

FIRE ON THEIR HEADS, BURNING SAND BELOW. THE HASTY RETREAT TURNS INTO A ROUT.

THIRST BEGINS TO TAKE ITS TOLL. STRAGGLERS ARE EASY PREY FOR THE KARANKAWAS, ALWAYS CLOSE BEHIND.

FINALLY COMING TO THE RIO BRAVO, THE SPANISH CROSS IN IMPROVISED RAFTS. ONLY WELL-PLACED BOLTS FROM THE CROSSBOWS KEEP THEIR PURSUERS AT BAY.

BELTS, ROPES, RAGS - WE NEED MORE LASHING!

ON THIS CROSSING A TRAGIC MISTAKE OCCURS. FRAY MENA, THINKING TO LIGHTEN HIS OVERLOADED RAFT, TOSSES A BUNDLE OVERBOARD. IT CONTAINS THE PRECIOUS CROSSBOWS.

WITH IT, THEIR HOPES SINK TO THE RIVER'S BOTTOM.

THE INDIANS FOLLOW, MORE DARING NOW AS THEY REALIZE THE FEARED WEAPONS ARE GONE.

FASTER AND FASTER RUN THE REFUGEES BUT IT IS NEVER ENOUGH TO ESCAPE THE KARANKAWAS' LONGBOWS.

A FEW, TOO PROUD TO ENDURE THE EMBARRASSMENT, ARE QUICKLY DISPATCHED BY THE SAVAGES WHO WAVE ALOFT THEIR BLOODY TROPHIES TO THE NAKED GROUP.

THE MISERABLE TREK CONTINUES, NOW EXPOSED TO AN INCREASINGLY HOSTILE TERRAIN.

EVEN SO, LUST BORN OF UNVEILED DELIGHTS — OR PERHAPS MADNESS — SLOWS THE PACE FOR SOME.

UTTERLY DISGUSTING..

DON DIEGO, LADY ISABELLA! HAVE YOU **NO** SHAME!?!

WHAT'S THE DIFFERENCE? IF WE DO, OR DON'T, WE DIE ANYWAY. YHAA-HAHAAA!

BEFORE THE PAIN, A LITTLE PLEASURE.. HE HE HE

AN INTOLERABLE SITUATION WHICH LEADS THE PRIESTS TO SEND THE WOMEN ON AHEAD, IN ORDER TO PRESERVE CHRISTIAN DECENCY.

GOD **SEES** WHAT WE DO HERE, EVEN IN THIS WILDERNESS, LET US ACT ACCORDINGLY!

IT SOON BECOMES APPARENT THAT THEIR RELENTLESS ENEMIES HAVE NOT GIVEN UP PURSUIT...

AND INDUCING THE SPANIARDS TO CAST OFF THEIR GARMENTS WAS ONLY A GUISE TO HUMILIATE THEM.

UHHH!

RUN! HERE THEY COME AGAIN!

HAHAHAAA

AS THE WOMEN REACH THE RIO de las PALMAS, PLACING THEM IN FRONT PROVES AN ILL-FOUNDED MEASURE.

FOR THERE OTHER INDIANS WAIT IN AMBUSH, AND THEY TAKE A TOLL ON MORE THAN CASTILIAN MODESTY.

WHEN THE MEN CATCH UP, NOT ONE OF THE GENTLER SEX OR ANY OF THE CHILDREN REMAIN ALIVE.

NOOOO..

JOSEFA! PABLITO..?? OH GOD!

LOOK WELL, PRIEST! THIS WAS OF YOUR MAKING!!

EXCEPT A FEW — PERHAPS BETTER OFF DEAD — DRAGGED TO THE MONTE FOR FIENDISH REASONS.

AMIDST THIS SAD SCENE, THE MASSACRE IS RENEWED.

UNTIL ONLY A HANDFUL ARE LEFT, ALL GRIEVIOUSLY WOUNDED. THEY CROSS THE RIVER AND SCATTER INTO THE BRUSH, EVERY MAN FOR HIMSELF.

RAMON! WE GO NOW OR WE ALL DIE!

STRUGGLING PITEOUSLY ONWARD, THEIR OPEN WOUNDS FESTER AND BECOME FLY BLOWN.

I.. I.. THINK THEY'VE GIVEN UP THE CHASE.

DON'T COUNT ON IT FATHER.

A NEGRESS, WHO HAD SOMEHOW ELUDED THE SAVAGES, CREEPS FROM HIDING TO NURSE HER FORMER MASTERS.

BE STRONG PADRE... IT'S COMING.

BLESS YOU MY CHILD— GROAN...

BUT OUT FORAGING ONE MORNING, SHE IS DISCOVERED.

DEAR GOD, IS THERE NO END TO IT?

WITHOUT HER HELP, FRAY MARCOS CANNOT CONTINUE. HE IS BURIED BY HIS COMPANIONS, BUT IN SUCH A WAY SO HE CAN BREATHE UNTIL DEATH COMES.

OOOH...

HE'S STILL ALIVE, JUST BARELY...

COVER HIS HEAD WITH WEEDS...

AND LET'S GO!

HE FALLS INTO AN EXHAUSTED SLEEP, SO DEEP THAT HE DOES NOT HEAR STEALTHY FEET PASS HIM BY.

WAKING, RESTORED BY THE SAND'S WARMTH, THE PRIEST CLAWS OUT OF HIS SHALLOW GRAVE AND STAGGERS ON.

SOON HE COMES UPON THE GHASTLY REMAINS OF THOSE WHO HAD LEFT HIM, THINKING TO ESCAPE THEIR MERCILESS TORMENTORS.

CHOKE...

IN HIS DELIRIUM EVERY BUSH BECOMES A CLUMP OF INDIANS BRISTLING WITH ARROWS TO INFLICT MORE PAIN.

CAN'T... LET... THEM... GET ME...

WHEN HE TRIES TO SLEEP, SAND CRABS COVER HIM, EATING THE MAGGOTS OUT OF HIS TORTURED FLESH.

YAAHH!!

FEVERISH FROM THIRST, AT LAST THE WEARY CLERIC REACHES A LARGE STREAM BUT ITS WATERS ARE TOO SALTY TO DRINK. IT IS THE LAST STRAW...

GAG!

SEEING INDIANS APPROACHING IN A CANOE, HE WELCOMES THE DEATH THAT THEY MOST CERTAINLY BRING.

INTROIBO AD ALTARE DEI...

BUT THESE ARE CIVILIZED, NOT HOSTILE, INDIANS. THEY BRING GOOD NEWS...

TAPICO...

GLUG GLUG

AND SET HIS FEET ON THE PATH OF DELIVERANCE.

HEHEHEHE... TAMPICO! HEHEHE

COLLAPSING OUTSIDE A VILLAGER'S HUT, AT LAST FRAY MARCOS' ORDEAL IS OVER.

DIOS! IT'S A PRIEST!! JUANA GO FETCH THE ALCALDE.

YEARS LATER FINDS HIM LIVING IN CLOISTERED SECLUSION IN A SMALL CONVENTO ROOM ATOP WHAT WAS ONCE CUZCO'S TEMPLE OF THE SUN.

AVE MARIA ♪♫♪

BUT THO RETIRED, FRAY MARCOS IS STILL HARD AT WORK, JUST AS HE HAS BEEN FOR THE PAST THIRTY YEARS!

I SEE HE'S AT IT AGAIN...

YES, WORKING ON HIS MURAL — SAFE IN THE ETERNAL BOSOM OF GOD!

THEY'RE COMING FOR ME, BUT... HE HE I'M NOT AFRAID...

KNOW WHY?

This is a true story, based on Fray Augustín Davila Padilla's account, published in 1560. Of the 300 shipwreck victims only Fray Marcos de Mena and one other Spaniard (who returned to the wreck site) survived.

END

C'MON, C'MON, LET'S LOOK ALIVE, PEOPLE. YOU'RE WAY BEHIND THE OTHERS!

YOYO PINTADO, SUB-SUPERINTENDENT OF MISSION ESPADA, TOLERATES NO FOOLISHNESS AT THE ANNUAL CORN HARVEST.

HE'S ONE PAJALACHE WHO FINALLY HAS THINGS GOING HIS WAY AND IS MAKING PROGRESS IN THIS WORLD.

YES, YOYO REPRESENTS THE HOPE OF THE FUTURE FOR ESPADA'S INDIAN POPULATION, ONLY A GENERATION REMOVED FROM BARBARIC SAVAGERY..

...SO DIFFERENT FROM THOSE WHO EMBRACE CHRISTIANITY, ONLY TO RENOUNCE IT AND RETURN TO THEIR WICKED WAYS..

FISCAL! SOME COASTAL RENEGADES ARE COMING.

WELL, WELL, LOOK AT THESE DUMB INDIANS, BUSTIN' THEIR ASS TO MAKE THE PRIESTS RICH.

YEAH, A REAL PATHETIC BUNCH, AIN'T THEY?

DON'T COME AROUND HERE, TRYIN' TO MESS THINGS UP FOR US. WE GOT THE GOOD LIFE..

YEAH.. DAT'S RIGHT

LIKE THOSE VICIOUS APOSTATES FORMERLY AT THE BAHÍA MISSIONS, WHO HATE NOTHING SO MUCH AS INDIANS CONTENT TO REMAIN DOMESTICATED.

THANK HEAVEN THAT SHINING EXAMPLES OF PIETY AND RECTITUDE — LIKE YOYO PINTADO — HAVE REWARDED THE MISSIONARIES' NOBLE EFFORTS!

HA! TH' GOOD LIFE IS DOWN ON TH' COAST. IT'LL BE EVEN BETTER WITH THIS PRETTY THING.

IF YOU WUSSIES EVER GET UP THE NERVE, COME 'N JOIN US!

EEEK!

TAKE CHARGE WHILE I GO TELL THE PADRE..

HAHAHA.. HHHELPP!!

MISSION ESPADA: SAFE HARBOR FOR THE VARIOUS TRIBAL GROUPS LIVING WITHIN ITS WALLS — LIKE YOYO'S PAJALACHES — OFFERING THEM AN OPPORTUNITY FOR SALVATION, CIVILIZATION, AND FULL TUMMY. IT IS A BOLD EXPERIMENT AND NOT ALL SPANIARDS SUBSCRIBE TO ITS UTOPIAN IDEALS...

THE GOOD LIFE

AS FISCAL PINTADO ENTERS THE MISSION COMPLEX HE REMEMBERS SOMETHING HE WAS SUPPOSED TO DELIVER TO HIS SUPERVISOR, FATHER CAMARENA.

IT IS UNUSUAL FOR YOYO TO RETURN FROM THE FIELDS SO EARLY.

DARN — I'D BETTER STOP BY THE HOUSE..

RITA, WHERE'D I PUT THAT LITTLE NOTEBOOK OF FATHER CA..

NOT ONLY UNUSUAL, BUT ON THIS DAY, QUITE *UNFORTUNATE*..

UH-OH..IT'S YOUR DUMBSHIT HUSBAND!

WHA?!

THE SCREAMS FROM THE PINTADO CUBICLE DRAW KNOWING SMILES FROM THEIR NEIGHBORS.

HEAR *THAT*? SOUNDS LIKE RITA TEMPTED FATE ONCE TOO OFTEN..

YEAH, UNTIL SHE FINALLY GOT CAUGHT!

AIEE! NO NU OUCH! YOWW! CRASH!

AS THE SHRIEKS GROW LOUDER, A CROWD GATHERS IN THE YARD.

THINK WE SHOULD GO SEE WHAT'S HAPPENING IN THERE?

NO WAY! THAT PUTA'S AFFAIRS ARE NONE OF MY BUSINESS AS LONG AS IT'S NOT MY CHICO SHE'S AFTER.

BIDE!! ARGGH! ASP

FINALLY THE COMMOTION SUBSIDES, BUT A GASP ESCAPES THE ONLOOKERS WHEN YOYO APPEARS.

DIOS! HE'S COVERED IN BLOOD!

CAREFUL... THERE'S A KNIFE IN HIS HAND!

YES, A BIG BUTCHER KNIFE, GIVEN TO HIM BY THE PRIEST AS A REWARD FOR LAST YEAR'S BOUNTIFUL HARVEST; HE SHARPENS IT EVERY EVENING, WITHOUT FAIL.

BACK, DAMN'D YOU! KEEP AWAY FROM ME, OR I'LL CUT YOU BAD!

YOYO BOLTS FOR THE NEAREST GATE AND THE THRONG FOLLOWS... BUT NOT TOO CLOSELY!

HE'S GETTING AWAY!

AFTER HIM!

OUTSIDE, YOYO — FRANTIC NOW — FINDS A SADDLED HORSE AND MANAGES TO CLIMB ON, NOVICE THO HE IS.

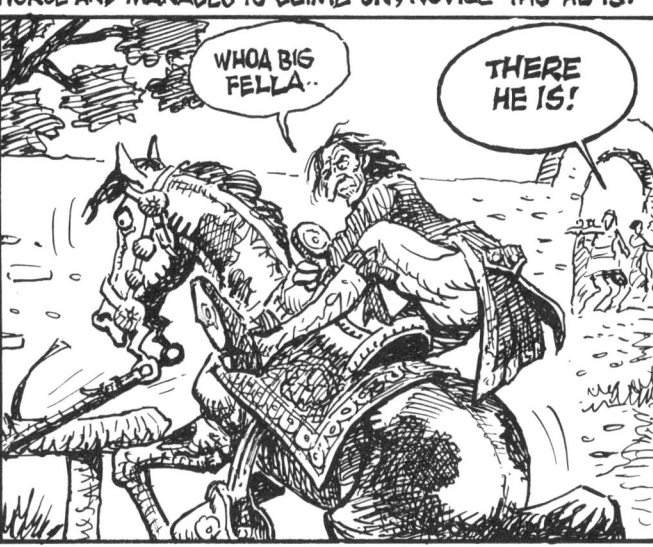

WHOA BIG FELLA..

THERE HE IS!

HAD HIS MIND NOT BEEN SO DISTRACTED HE WOULD HAVE RECOGNIZED THE PINTO PONY AS BELONGING TO A VAQUERO FROM THE COASTAL MISSION, A DARK, SWARTHY FELLOW WITH THE REPUTATION OF A LADIES' MAN.

GUESS WE'LL NEVER CATCH HIM NOW...

HMPH! I'M NOT SURE I'D WANT TO CATCH A KNIFE-TOTING LUNATIC.

MEANWHILE, SEVERAL WOMEN APPROACH THE DEATHLY-QUIET PINTADO HOUSEHOLD.

YOU CAN COME OUT NOW RITA, HE'S GONE. RITA..??

THEIR NEWLY-CHRISTIANIZED NERVES ARE NOT READY FOR THE SIGHT THAT ASSAULTS THEM.

AAIIEEE

FETCH THE PRIEST, QUICK!

WE MUST PRAY..

YOYO WAS PRAYING TOO — PRAYING THAT THEY DIDN'T CATCH HIM! HE WHIPPED THE PAINT HORSE MERCILESSLY ONWARD.

IT WAS TOO DANGEROUS TO TRAVEL THE BAHIA ROAD. HE MIGHT MEET SOME SOLDIERS WHO WOULD WANT TO SEE HIS PASS, QUESTION HIS RIGHT TO BE AWAY FROM THE MISSION.

SO HE KEPT OFF THE BEATEN PATH UNTIL THE BRUSH GOT TOO THICK TO CONTINUE..

HIS FINE COAT WAS HANGING IN TATTERS BEFORE HE REACHED THE MEDINA RIVER.

STILL HE RODE ON, LOOKING BEHIND HIM LESS FREQUENTLY NOW.

THE FRIGHTENED PAJALACHE KEPT RIDING UNTIL HE REALIZED HE DIDN'T KNOW WHERE HE WAS GOING. THEN HE PAUSED TO LOOK AROUND HIM. A BEAUTIFUL TWILIGHT WAS SETTLING UPON THE LAND; IT WOULD BE DARK SOON. HAD TO *THINK*, TO PLAN HIS ESCAPE. IT WOULDN'T DO TO BE RUNNING AROUND IN THE WOODS AT NIGHT. EVIL SPIRITS MIGHT BE AFOOT. YOYO SHUDDERED AT MEMORIES OF THAT AWFUL SCENE BACK IN THE BLOOD-SPATTERED ROOM.

HE WHEELED THE PAINT HORSE AND RETRACED HIS STEPS TO THE RUINS HE'D PASSED BACK ON SKULL CREEK.

HIDING HIS HORSE IN THE BUSHES JUST AS DARKNESS FELL, YOYO CREPT TO THE GUTTED, ABANDONED BUILDING.

HE COLLAPSED BENEATH A LOWER WINDOW, WHERE HE'D BE SURE TO HEAR APPROACHING HOOFBEATS.

THE STARS BEGAN TWINKLING AS YOYO EXAMINED HIS CHANCES. HE WASN'T SORRY FOR WHAT HE'D DONE THAT AFTERNOON—A LITTLE SCARED, PERHAPS, BUT NOT SORRY.

NO, THAT MAN—WHOEVER HE WAS—DESERVED TO HAVE HIS THROAT CUT.

AND HIS ADULTEROUS WIFE, SHE'D DESERVED HERS TOO.

"TELL ME THE TRUTH," HE'D SAID, "AND I'LL SPARE YOU." SO SHE FOOLISHLY ADMITTED THAT HIS DAUGHTER AND THE CHILD SHE CARRIED BELONGED TO THE STRANGER IN HIS HOUSE, THE DEAD MAN GURGLING ON THE FLOOR. IT DIDN'T MATTER NOW; HE'D FIXED THEM ALL. THEN YOYO REMEMBERED THE BULGE IN HIS COAT-POCKET.

HE TOOK OUT THE TROPHIES AND EXAMINED THEM CURIOUSLY IN THE MOONLIGHT, WONDERING IF THEY MIGHT SERVE AS A NECKLACE ORNAMENT OF SORTS.

PROBABLY NOT.. THEY DIDN'T HAVE ANY KIND OF BONE INSIDE LIKE A FINGER DID. HE TOSSED THE USELESS ITEMS ON THE FLOOR AND CONSIDERED HIS SITUATION.

PLOP

HE COULD NEVER GO BACK TO ESPADA, OR ANY OTHER MISSION... MUCH TOO DANGEROUS. SOONER OR LATER HE'D BE LINKED WITH YOYO PINTADO, THE ESCAPED KILLER. THAT WAS A SHAME. JUST WHEN LIFE WAS GOING HIS WAY... HE CURSED HIS FAITHLESS WIFE, REMEMBERING ALL THE TIMES HE'D COME HOME TO FIND HER GONE. WELL, HE'D BEEN TOO BUSY TO DO OTHER THAN TRUST HER — TRYING TO GET AHEAD, TO IMPROVE HIMSELF. A WOMAN WAS SUPPOSED TO HELP, TO COMFORT HER MAN AND BRUSH AWAY WORRISOME THINGS... BUT RITA HADN'T HELPED; SHE'D RUINED HIM, COST HIM HIS JOB, AND GOTTEN HIM IN A HELL OF A FIX. HE WISHED HE'D HAD TIME TO MAKE HER PAY FOR HER SINS IN PROPER FASHION, THE LOW-DOWN, DECEIVING BITCH..

WHAT NOW? YOYO PULLED HIS TORN COAT CLOSER ABOUT HIM, SHIVERING IN THE AUTUMN NIGHT'S CHILL. IT WAS TOO RISKY TO BUILD A FIRE. HIS HAT — HE'D LOST HIS AWE-INSPIRING HAT. DAMMIT! AND THE OTHER THINGS HE'D HAD TO LEAVE BEHIND, LIKE HIS SERAPE. THAT INCONSIDERATE WHORE, RUINING EVERYTHING..

THEN THE NIGHTTIME SYMPHONY BEGAN. WOLVES BEGAN TO HOWL, THE SOUND OF THE PACK COMING NEARER. A PANTHER SCREAMED FROM THE HILL ABOVE.

CHRIST, THERE WERE *WILD BEASTS* IN THESE WOODS AS WELL AS EVIL SPIRITS! YOYO HAD BEEN BORN AND RAISED IN A MISSION; HE DIDN'T KNOW ANYTHING ABOUT ROUGHING IT. OH SURE, HE'D HEARD THE OLD PEOPLE TALK ABOUT LIFE IN THE STICKS BUT IT HAD SEEMED LIKE A FAIRY TALE, LIKE STORIES THE PRIESTS TOLD. MISSION INDIANS WERE ALWAYS INSIDE THE WALLS OF THE COMPOUND BEFORE DARK, SAFE FROM PROWLING THINGS IN THE WILD.

HE STARTED. FOOTSTEPS WERE SOFTLY CRUNCHING THE TURF OUTSIDE THIS ANCIENT WALL. WHATEVER IT WAS OUT THERE WOULD SOON BE REACHING THE WINDOW.

YOYO SWALLOWED HARD AND CROUCHED ON THE FLOOR EXPECTING SATAN TO STICK HIS HORNED HEAD INTO THE ROOM AT ANY MOMENT. HIS HEART WAS POUNDING.

CRUNCH
CRUNCH

THE SHUFFLING NOISE STOPPED.

AGAINST HIS WILL YOYO PEERED UP...

DIOS, IT WAS SATAN!!

YOYO SCRAMBLED TO HIS FEET AND FLED, NEVER DARING TO LOOK BACK.

IMAGINE, THEN, THE PANIC OF THE BILLY GOAT THAT HAD UNWITTINGLY POKED ITS HEAD INTO THE WINDOW, LOOKING FOR A SUITABLE PLACE TO SPEND THE NIGHT!

YOYO CHARGED OUT OF THE RUINS, STUMBLING OVER ROCKS AND CACTUS. IT WAS A FOOLISH THING TO DO.

THE HORSE, ALREADY SKITTISH BECAUSE OF THE PANTHER'S SCREAMS, BOLTED AT ALL THE COMMOTION IN THE DARK.

IT WRENCHED ITS REINS FREE AND THUNDERED OFF, HEADING DOWN THE ROAD TOWARD THE COAST AND HOME.

CONVINCED THAT WHATEVER MONSTER HAD BEEN IN THE STABLE WAS NOW IN HOT PURSUIT, THE TERRIFIED GOAT ABANDONED THE BAHIA ROAD FOR THE BRUSH, BLEATING AS IT WENT. THE HOVERING WOLF PACK CLOSED IN...

MEANWHILE, YOYO WAS ON THE VERGE OF INSANITY. HE COWERED IN THE MESQUITE SCRUBS, ANXIOUSLY SCANNING THE RUINS TO SEE IF EL DIABLO WAS STILL THERE. MAYBE SATAN HAD DECIDED TO GO AFTER THE HORSE INSTEAD OF YOYO PINTADO.

GODDAMN THAT RITA — WHAT A BIND SHE'D PUT HIM IN! STUCK OUT HERE IN THIS AWFUL PLACE, CRAWLING WITH FIENDISH GHOULS... NOW HE WAS STRANDED ON FOOT!

HORRIBLE SOUNDS WERE COMING FROM THE ARROYO CALAVERAS. THE DEVIL HAD CAUGHT HIS PAINT HORSE AND WAS DRAGGING IT TOWARD THE PORTALS OF HELL.

ITS CRIES WERE SO AGONIZINGLY PITIFUL THAT IT DIDN'T EVEN SOUND LIKE A HORSE ANYMORE.

BBAAAAAA

AFTER AN ETERNITY THE RACKET STOPPED AND YOYO CLIMBED A TREE, TO BE SAFE FROM THINGS THAT SLITHERED ON THE GROUND. OF COURSE IT WAS IMPOSSIBLE TO GET ANY SLEEP, SO HE SPENT THE HOURS TRYING TO FIGURE OUT WHY HIS LIFE HAD SUDDENLY TURNED TO SHIT. THERE HAD TO BE AN EXPLANATION.

WHAT WAS IT THE PRIESTS SAID? "THOU SHALT NOT KILL." MAYBE THAT WAS THE REASON. BUT THEY ALSO SAID "AN EYE FOR AN EYE" AND HAD A LONG LIST OF OTHER THINGS A PERSON SHOULD OR SHOULD NOT DO. IT WAS ALL TERRIBLY CONFUSING. SOONER OR LATER MERE MORTALS WERE BOUND TO MESS UP, ESPECIALLY IF THEY WERE MERE INDIAN MORTALS! ONLY SPANISH PRIESTS SEEMED ABLE TO LIVE BY THE RULES..

THEN THE ANSWER CAME TO YOYO: HE WOULD JOIN SOME BAND OF WILD AND CRAZY APOSTATE INDIANS. THEY WOULDN'T LET THE PRIESTS GET HIM. *FUCK THE PRIESTS ANYWAY*— HE WAS TIRED OF BEING THEIR SLAVE. "YOYO DO THIS, YOYO DO THAT" ALL TH' TIME. WELL, HE'D BE A FREE MAN AND HAVE SOME FUN FOR A CHANGE !!

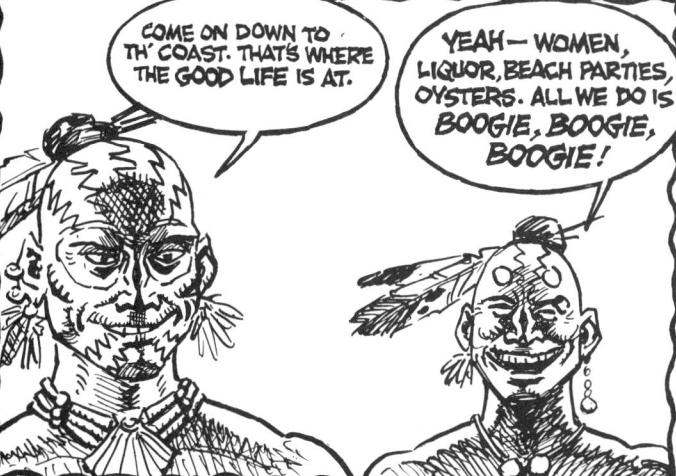  

jaxon·89

THE SAVAGE WITHIN

PLACIDO GUTIERREZ *HI-YAAD* AT HIS BONY COWS, TRYING TO GET THEM BUNCHED UP SO THE BASTARDS WOULDN'T BOLT WHEN THEY REACHED THE MISSION GATE.

THIS WAS HIS BRIEF MOMENT IN THE LIMELIGHT, WHEN HIS IMPORTANCE TO MISSION ESPADA COULD NOT BE DENIED. THAT IDIOT FISCAL, YOYO PINTADO, MIGHT STRUT ABOUT AND GIVE ORDERS BUT IT TOOK A REAL MAN TO PUT MEAT ON THE TABLE.

FRAY CAMARENA, TRAILED BY AN EXCITED GROUP OF CHILDREN, WAS ON HAND TO WATCH THE GRAND PROCESSION.

BEFORE THE PRIEST COULD INSPECT HIS PRECIOUS CARGO OF BEEF, A WOMAN'S SCREAMS MADE HIM STOP AND TURN.

GO FIND THE FISCAL. TELL HIM THE COWS ARE HERE.

PADRE, PADRE, A TERRIBLE THING! COME QUICKLY—SHE'S DYING!!

SHE WAS BESIDE HERSELF WITH TERROR..BLOOD STAINED HER DRESS.

WHAT IS IT, MY CHILD? WHO'S DYING? WHO?

THE WIFE OF YOYO PINTADO, YOUR GRACE. STABBED WITH A KNIFE.. ≥SOB≤ JUST AWFUL!!

FATHER JOSEF RUSHED TOWARD THE PINTADO HUT ALONG THE SOUTH WALL.

EVERYBODY ELSE IN THE MISSION HEADED THERE TOO, THE COWS NOW FORGOTTEN.

WHAT COULD BE OF GREATER INTEREST THAN HIS COWS? PLACIDO WATCHED THE MASS EXODUS WITH AMAZEMENT.

!

HE SPAT INTO THE DUST, JABBING HIS HORSE WITH WICKED SPURS.

PROBABLY YOYO'S DOING.. THAT DUMB PAJALACHE, ALWAYS TRYIN' TO STEAL TH' SHOW!

THE WEATHERED OLD FOREMAN COULD NOT HAVE BEEN MORE CORRECT.

STAND ASIDE! MAKE WAY!!

A HORRIBLE SIGHT GREETED THE PRIEST INSIDE THE FISCAL'S APARTMENT, A SIGHT THAT HIS BRIEF TENURE ON THE NORTHERN FRONTIER HAD NOT PREPARED HIM FOR.

..GOD IN HEAVEN..

THERE WERE THREE BODIES IN THE WRECKED ROOM — FOUR, IF YOU COUNTED THE SHAPELESS LUMP AGAINST THE FAR WALL.

THE FISCAL LAY FACE DOWN ON THE FLOOR, A HASTILY-DONNED SHIRT HALFWAY ON...

BESIDE HIM WAS HIS LITTLE DAUGHTER, CRUEL STAB WOUNDS PUNCTURING HER FRAIL TORSO.

THEY WERE BOTH DEAD, BUT THE RAVAGED FORM IN THE BACK CORNER YET BREATHED.

IT WAS RITA PINTADO, THE FISCAL'S YOUNG WIFE, WHO LAY WELTERING IN HER OWN GORE ON THE PALLET THAT SERVED AS THE FAMILY BED.

UUUUUH

AT LEAST IT APPEARED TO BE HER. WHAT HAD ONCE BEEN AN ATTRACTIVE, BUXOM WOMAN WAS HARDLY NOW RECOGNIZABLE AS SUCH..

RITA??

SHE CLUTCHED A GAPING HOLE IN HER ABDOMEN, ARMS QUIVERING, COVERED IN BLOOD TO THE ELBOWS.

GGGA-URK

THE PRIEST STEPPED ON ONE OF HER SEVERED BREASTS IN THE DIM LIGHT.

SQUISHH

RITA DID NOT SEE HIM. HER EYES WERE ALREADY SET ON THE COMING VISTA OF DEATH.

MY CHILD, WHO DID THIS TERRIBLE THING TO YOU? WHO??

HER LIPS PARTED AND SHE MADE A DEEP, RASPING SOUND THAT TRAILED OFF INTO A GUTTURAL MOAN..

FATHER JOSEF COULDN'T MAKE IT OUT. SINCE THE POOR WOMAN WAS OBVIOUSLY BEYOND CONFESSION, HE COULD ONLY PERFORM THE SACRAMENT OF EXTREME UNCTION.

YOOAAA

THERE WASN'T TIME TO FETCH HIS OILS TO DO IT RIGHT. THINGS WERE NEVER AS THEY SHOULD BE IN THIS VIOLENT LAND, NOT EVEN WITH FINAL RITES.

ALMOST BEFORE HE FINISHED, RITA PINTADO WAS GONE...

STILL ON HIS KNEES, FATHER JOSEF TURNED TO SURVEY THE SCENE OF THE DREADFUL CRIME: SOME DERANGED MANIAC HAD COME INTO THE FISCAL'S HOUSE AND BUTCHERED ITS OCCUPANTS — THE WHOLE FAMILY, MURDERED WHILE TAKING A LATE SIESTA!

FINALLY THE PRIEST BECAME AWARE OF ALL THE PEOPLE PACKED AROUND THE OPEN DOOR, PEERING IN AT THE ABATTOIR AND SPEAKING IN HUSHED WHISPERS.

GO AWAY, MY CHILDREN! THE DEVIL HAS BEEN HERE.

LEAVE, OR THE EVIL WILL BLAST YOUR SOULS! GO PRAY IN THE CHURCH!

SLAM

ZOMBIE-LIKE HE WALKED THROUGH THE CARNAGE. THEN HE FELL ON HIS KNEES AGAIN, HIS PRAYERS DROWNING OUT THE BUZZ FROM THE CELL'S SMALL WINDOW.

OH LORD, WHY YOU ALLOW SUCH THINGS TO HAPPEN IS HARD FOR US TO UNDERSTAND...

WHEN TWO MEN ENTERED THEY FOUND HIM STILL BE-SIDE THE BLOODY REMAINS OF THE FISCAL'S FAMILY.

YOUNG FATHER GARCIA TOOK ONE LOOK AND BOLTED FOR THE DOOR, BUT THE OTHER WAS MADE OF STERNER STUFF.

UURP..

FRANCISCO ROJAS, THE MISSION SUPERINTENDENT, CLOSED THE DOOR AND LOOKED AROUND. HE SAW THE WOMAN'S BODY, THE WHITE-WASHED WALLS ABOVE HER SPLATTERED AND SMEARED WITH BLOOD, LIKE SHE HAD COWERED THERE, BEGGING FOR MERCY WHILE HER ATTACKER WORKED.

ROJAS WAS NO STRANGER TO SCENES OF VIOLENCE. HIS SPECIALTY HAD BEEN FALLING UPON THE ENEMY'S SLEEPING CAMPS. BUT THAT WAS A LONG TIME AGO..

I FIGURED SOMETHING LIKE THIS WOULD HAPPEN!

FRAY CAMARENA SMILED, THANKFUL FOR THE PRESENCE OF ANOTHER LIVING SOUL IN A ROOM TAINTED WITH SO MUCH DEATH.

FRANCISCO, MY SON..

SOONER OR LATER IT WAS BOUND TO HAPPEN, PADRE.

TOO MANY TIMES THAT COWBOY FROM THE COASTAL MISSION HAS DARED TO COME UP HERE, OPENLY MEETING WITH FISCAL PINTADO'S WIFE..

WHAT!!? A HOLY GHOST INDIAN KILLED POOR YOYO? I..I DON'T...

ELISCO GRUNTED AND MOTIONED TO THE VAQUERO GEAR PILED ON THE LOW STOOL.

NO FATHER, THAT AIN'T YOYO — IT'S THAT LOW-LIFE JARANAME VAQUERO FROM ESPIRITU SANTO!

THE PRIEST, NOT UNDERSTANDING, TURNED TO THE MALE CORPSE ON THE DIRT FLOOR.

EH?

WHAT FRANCISCO SAID WAS TRUE.

YAAA!

THUD

THE MISSIONARY RECOILED IN HORROR, REELING, SLIPPING, AND LOSING HIS BALANCE IN THE LARGE POOL OF BLOOD THAT SEEPED FROM UNDER THE DEAD MAN'S BUTTOCKS.

YEAH, THAT'S CASI LOCO. PLUMB CRAZY, YOUR EMINENCE.. ALWAYS FOOLING AROUND WITH OTHER MEN'S WIVES..

FATHER JOSEF WAS IN SHOCK..

HOW LONG HAS THIS BEEN GOING ON FRANCISCO?

OH, FOR A LONG TIME PADRE.. I THINK YOYO MUST HAVE FINALLY GOTTEN WISE.. OR MAYBE HE JUST BLUNDERED INTO IT.

IF THE PRIEST WAS HAVING TROUBLE STRUCTURING THE DAY'S EVENTS, ROJAS COULD SEE THEM WITH CLARITY. RITA HAD KNOWN THAT ON SATURDAY HER HUSBAND WOULD BE KEPT BUSY IN THE FIELDS AND DOWN AT THE CORRAL, WHEN THE CATTLE ARRIVED.

SHE HAD INVITED HER LOVER HERE, RATHER THAN MEETING HIM AT THE CREEK AS SHE USUALLY DID.

YOU CRAZY MAN!

THEY WERE ENGAGED IN SEX, THE LITTLE GIRL PLAYING ON THE FLOOR BESIDE THEM.

UHHH!! AHH-AHHH!! UMM-UHH!

BUT YOYO UNEXPECTEDLY CAME HOME; IF CASI'S BODY WERE ROLLED OVER, DOUBTLESS HIS GENITALS WOULD BE MISSING.

THEN HE HEMMED HIS UNFAITHFUL WIFE IN THE CORNER AND CURSED HER FOR A WHORE.

THE BABY, IT'S HIS ISN'T IT? AND THE NIÑA OVER THERE, HIS TOO?!? TELL ME THE TRUTH, WOMAN!

SHE HAD LIED AND IT SENT YOYO INTO A RAGE. HE WAS LIKE THAT, TOO JEALOUS; TOO PROUD TO LET IT GO BY..

'CISCO NOTICED THE BLOODY SPLATTER ON THE FAR WALL, TRICKLING DOWN TO A MELON-SIZED BLOB ON THE FLOOR.

SO YOYO HAD RIPPED THE UNBORN CHILD FROM RITA'S WOMB AND FLUNG IT ACROSS THE ROOM. THEN HE'D DONE THE REST..

A DREADFUL THING BUT THE OLD SUPER HAD SEEN IT BEFORE; PAJALACHES WERE LIKE THAT, MEAN AND VICIOUS WHEN RILED.

FRAY CAMARENA WAS STILL STRUGGLING WITH THE REALIZATION THAT IT WAS NOT YOYO LYING DEAD ON THE FLOOR.

WHY WASN'T I TOLD ABOUT THIS.. THIS INDIAN FROM ANOTHER MISSION, COMING HERE TO DISTURB OUR COMMUNITY..?

ROJAS SHRUGGED. HE KNEW THAT YOU DID NOT MESS IN ANOTHER MAN'S DOMESTIC AFFAIRS. IT WAS NOT THE INDIAN WAY. NO, THE FISCAL'S WRETCHED LOVE LIFE WAS NOT HIS PROBLEM.

BUT OF COURSE THE REVEREND FATHER DIDN'T THINK ABOUT IT IN A REASONABLE WAY. HE ACTED LIKE EVERYONE'S BUSINESS AT THE MISSION WAS HIS BUSINESS TOO, ESPECIALLY THEIR MORALS.

THIS.. THIS BED OF INIQUITY... WHY WASN'T I TOLD?

THE PRIEST WAS OVERWHELMED TO THINK THAT, ALL THIS TIME, HE'D BEEN OBLIVIOUS TO THE DARK, SINISTER URGES INSIDE HIS HAND-PICKED REPRESENTATIVE, YOYO PINTADO.

HE SEEMED LIKE SUCH A NICE FELLOW, BRIGHT, WELL MANNERED, A HARD WORKER.. WHO WOULD HAVE THOUGHT.?

RITES OF EXORCISM ARE NEEDED TO DRIVE THE EVIL FROM THIS ROOM. THEN WE MUST WHITE-WASH THE WALLS AND LOCK IT UP!

OUTSIDE THE FISCAL'S DOOR NO ONE HAD LEFT. DETAILS OF THE MACABRE SPECTACLE SPREAD LIKE WILDFIRE.

HIS COWS PENNED, PLACIDO GUTIERREZ STROLLED OVER JUST IN TIME TO SEE ROJAS AND THE PRIEST EMERGE FROM YOYO'S HUT.

IT WASN'T TH' FIRST TIME..

HE HAD IT COMING..

..DOWN BY THE CREEK..

AND THE HARLOT AS WELL..

WHERE IS THE FISCAL PINTADO?

JUST AS HE'D FIGURED: THAT CHICKENSHIT FISCAL HAD PULLED SOME KIND OF STUNT TO ECLIPSE HIS ONE DAY OF GLORY!

I SAW HIM HEAD FOR THAT GATE, WAVIN' A BLOODY KNIFE!

HE'S LONG GONE, YOUR GRACE. YOU'LL NEVER CATCH HIM!

PLACIDO COULD CATCH HIM, PROBABLY THE ONLY MAN AT THE MISSION THAT COULD. BUT HE DIDN'T WANT TO GO OUT AND ROPE SOME CRAZY PAJALACHE WITH A FETISH FOR BUTCHER KNIVES.

..RODE OFF ON A PAINT HORSE..

NO, PLACIDO GUTIERREZ COULD THINK OF MORE PLEASANT WAYS TO SPEND THE EVENING. HE MELTED INTO THE SHADOWS ALONG THE WALL LEST FATHER CAMARENA SHOULD NOTICE HIM...

Jaxon·89

END

POSSUM ON A STICK

TIME WAS WHEN A PAJALACHE COULD RUN FOR DAYS WITHOUT END. BUT THAT WAS BEFORE THE TRIBE GAVE UP THE CHASE AND ACCEPTED MISSION LIFE, BEFORE THEY ALLOWED THEIR BODIES TO BECOME SO SOFT.

THUS, YOYO PINTADO WAS ALREADY DEAD TIRED WHEN HE REACHED THE CIBOLO. HE KNEW HE'D NEVER MAKE IT TO THE COAST ON FOOT. NO, HE'D GOTTEN TOO SOFT; HIS ONLY CHANCE FOR ESCAPE WAS DOWN IN THAT SPANISH CORRAL.

HE WISHED THAT HE KNEW MORE ABOUT HORSES, HOW TO PICK A GOOD ONE FROM THOSE THAT WEREN'T SO GOOD..

BUT HE DIDN'T. AT ESPADA THE TACAMES WERE THE HORSEY SET. HIS PEOPLE MOSTLY DUG DITCHES & PICKED COTTON.

SHIT...

USING A PIECE OF DISCARDED ROPE YOYO MANAGED TO CORNER AND LOOP A SCRUBBY LITTLE DUN MUSTANG.

HOLD STILL, LITTLE HORSEY. HE HE HE HE

IT WAS THE ONLY HORSE THAT ALLOWED ITSELF TO BE CAUGHT, SO IT WOULD HAVE TO DO...

SO FAR, SO GOOD..

?!?

JUST AS YOYO FOUND THE CORRAL GATE, A DOG STARTED BARKING UP AT THE RANCH HOUSE.

GGRR GGGGRRRR WUOO WOO WOO

HE FUMBLED WITH THE POLES; THE BARKING INTENSIFIED.

C'MON, DAMMIT!

SOFT FEET GLIDED TO-WARD HIM IN THE DARK.

BARELY HAD HE FLUNG HIMSELF UPON THE DOCILE PONY'S BACK THAN THE MUTT SPRANG AT HIS LEG, SNARLING SAVAGELY.

RAURGG

INSIDE THE HOUSE DIEGO GORTARI HAD BEEN HALF LISTENING TO JOSEFA'S TOUGH OLD PET DOG. "YELLER" WAS ALWAYS BARKING AT SOME KIND OF VARMINT, ALL DURING THE NIGHT.

BUT THEN THE BARKING HEADED TOWARD THE CORRAL, LOUDER AS IT WENT. MIGHT BE THAT PANTHER, COME BACK AGAIN FOR THE FOAL.

DIEGO ONLY HAD TIME TO LEVEL HIS GUN AT THE SOUND OF HOOVES BEARING DOWN ON HIM.

IT WAS HIS FAVORITE SADDLE HORSE, "SLEEPY," WITH A RIDER CROUCHING LOW ON HIS NECK.

STOP THIEF! STOP, OR I'LL SHOOT!

AS SLEEPY ROARED BY, DIEGO CAUGHT A GLIMPSE OF PANTALOONS AND COATTAILS FLAPPING.

OUT OF FRUSTRATION HE FIRED HIS SHOTGUN INTO THE AIR ABOVE THE BOLD LADRÓN.

WELL OF ALL TH' NERVE!

★!!③!★!!

BOOM

THE BOOM AND DIEGO'S CURSES BROUGHT THE WIDOW GUERRA'S HOUSE TO LIFE.

WHAT'S GOING ON, DIEGO? WHY DID YOU FIRE YOUR GUN?

SOME SONUVA-BITCH HAS JUST MADE OFF WITH MY HORSE!!

I WOULD'VE KILLED THE BASTARD BUT WAS AFRAID I'D HIT SLEEPY IN THE DARK!

GORTARI WAS OVERWROUGHT.

GOD-DAMMIT! IN TH' DEAD OF NIGHT, WHEN YOU'D THINK MOST WHITE MEN WOULD BE HOME ASLEEP IN BED.

A WHITE MAN? SURELY NOT...

YES MY DEAR, I SAW HIS CLOTHES, SPANISH GARB—NOT SOMETHING A SKULKING INDIAN WOULD WEAR!

WHUMP

YOU'LL NOT GET AWAY WITH IT! THAT'S MY HORSE AND BY GOD I'LL HAVE HIM BACK!

·76·

FOUR DAYS LATER YOYO PINTADO SAT ROASTING A POSSUM IN A MESQUITE THICKET NEAR THE DEFUNCT MISSION ROSARIO.

HE'D JUST HAD HIS FIRST GOOD NIGHT'S SLEEP SINCE THIS MAD ADVENTURE BEGAN. THE HUTS AT ROSARIO WERE MUCH LIKE ESPADA'S, BUT IT WAS TOO RISKY THERE IN THE DAYTIME.

KOFF KOFFF

A GOOD REST AND NOW A GOOD MEAL; THINGS WERE BEGINING TO GO RIGHT FOR HIM AT LAST.

COUGH UGH COU

POP FIZZ

SIZZLE BPPSS

HE WONDERED HOW LONG HE'D HAVE TO KEEP HIDING IN THE BUSHES BEFORE SOME APOSTATE INDIAN HAPPENED BY. NOT LONG, HE HOPED. THIS WAS DEFINITELY NOT THE GOOD LIFE HE'D COME ALL THE WAY DOWN HERE TO FIND.

HACK COUGH HOUPP CHOKE

JUST AS YOYO WAS READY TO TAKE HIS BREAKFAST OFF THE SMOLDERING FIRE HE HEARD AN OMINOUS NOISE BEHIND HIM.

CLICK

WHIRLING AROUND HE SAW A FIERCE-LOOKING MAN WITH A *BIG GUN*, AIMED RIGHT AT HIS HEAD.

SO YOU'RE NOT A SPANIARD AFTER ALL, JUST SOME DAMNED INDIAN. DO YOU SPEAK THE KING'S TONGUE, ROGUE?

OOH SEÑOR, PLEASE DON'T SHOOT ME. I AM A CHRISTIAN, A GOOD INDIAN...

DIEGO NODDED TO HIS DUN MUSTANG TIED IN THE THICKET.

NOT VERY GOOD AT STEALING SPANISH HORSES THO' ARE YOU? THAT ONE OVER THERE IS MINE!

YOYO'S EYES WIDENED IN TERROR. IT WAS USELESS TO TRY AND BULLSHIT HIS WAY OUT OF THIS MESS.

UH-OH... HE'S BEEN ON MY TRAIL EVER SINCE THAT CORRAL

IN THE NAME OF THE BLESSED SAVIOR, LET ME EAT BEFORE YOU TAKE ME IN. LOOK, THERE'S MY MEAT ON THE FIRE...

SINCE IT WAS YOYO'S POSSUM HE MOVED FIRST. HASTY OF HIM...

SWOOSH

THUNK

BUT DIEGO WAS ALSO HASTY. INSTEAD OF SPLITTING YOYO'S HEAD LIKE A MELON, THE SCOUT'S MACHETE GLANCED OFF HIS THICK SKULL, MERELY CLEAVING AN EAR.

YOWWW!!

YOYO GINGERLY PICKED HIS EAR OUT OF THE DIRT AND, CHILD-LIKE, TRIED TO STICK IT BACK ON HIS HEAD.

EACH TIME IT PLOPPED TO THE GROUND HE HOWLED ANEW.

THE OLD SCOUT SQUATTED, PICKED UP THE SMOKING POSSUM, AND SCRAPED AWAY THE CHARRED FLESH.

HAD DIEGO GORTARI KNOWN OF YOYO'S MONSTROUS DOINGS BACK AT MISSION ESPADA, DOUBTLESS HE WOULD HAVE FINISHED HIM OFF RIGHT THERE IN THE BRUSH. BUT DIEGO HAD ACCOMPLISHED HIS OBJECTIVES: HIS BELOVED MUSTANG WAS BACK SAFE AND SOUND, THE CULPRIT SAT HUMBLED IN THE DUST AT HIS FEET, AND BREAKFAST WAS READY.

SO HE PROCEEDED TO HAVE A LEISURELY MEAL, EYE-ING THE VANQUISHED INDIAN WITH INDIFFERENCE...

DESPITE HIS PAIN YOYO'S MOUTH WATERED AS HE WATCHED BITE AFTER BITE OF HIS PRECIOUS POSSUM DISAPPEAR INTO THE SPANIARD'S MOUTH.

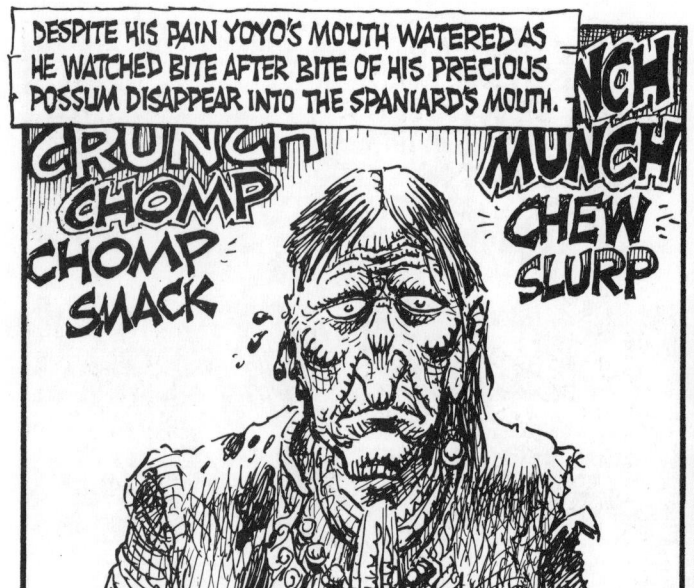

HE AVERTED HIS EYES, SINKING LOWER INTO THE DIRT. YES, IT WAS ALL THAT DAMNED RITA'S FAULT...

AT LENGTH DIEGO FINISHED AND TOSSED THE CARCASS ASIDE. THEN HE SETTLED BACK AND ROLLED HIMSELF A SMOKE.

HOW COME YOU PICKED MY HORSE TO STEAL? OF ALL THE HORSES IN TEXAS, WHY DID YOU TAKE MY SLEEPY?

TELL ME THAT, LADRÓN.

THE SCOUT GRINNED AND WAITED FOR AN ANSWER. HE WAS IN NO HURRY.

JUST MY LUCK, I SUPPOSE. THINGS HAVE BEEN GOING BAD FOR ME LATELY, SEÑOR.

THE REASON I TOOK YOUR HORSE WAS TO GET BACK QUICKLY TO MY HOME. BUT I ARRIVED TOO LATE; MY CHERISHED WIFE AND LITTLE GIRL HAD ALREADY PASSED AWAY.

DEAD, SEÑOR... I HAVE :SOB: LOST MUCH THESE LAST FEW DAYS :SNIFF:

DIEGO REPLIED GOOD NATUREDLY..

YES, IT IS A TERRIBLE THING TO LOSE LOVED ONES. AND NOW YOU HAVE LOST AN EAR AS WELL..

BUT AT LEAST YOU STILL POSSESS YOUR WORTHLESS LIFE. BE THANKFUL FOR THE SMALL THINGS IN THIS WORLD, LADRÓN.

YOYO WAS DISCONSOLATE. HE KNEW IT WAS NO GOOD TRYING TO ESCAPE. THE COUNTRY WAS TOO OPEN AROUND HERE; IF HE RAN, THIS RUDE FELLOW WOULD ONLY FIND HIM AND HUMILIATE HIM FURTHER.

ISN'T THAT RIGHT? HAHA HAHAHA HAH

HE STARED FORLORNLY AT HIS EAR. FLIES WERE ON IT AND THE BLOOD WAS STARTING TO CAKE.

BUZZZ BUZZZ BUZZZ ZZZ

THE SCENE IN HIS HOUSE CAME BACK TO HIM— THE MUTILATED BODIES, ALL THE GORE. YOYO TRIED TO SORT THINGS OUT BUT DIDN'T KNOW WHERE TO BEGIN.

Jaxon·90

END

THE COLT REVOLVER and the TEXAS RANGERS

TEXAS DURING ITS DECADE AS A REPUBLIC WAS BESET BY MEXICAN INVASIONS AND CONSTANT INDIAN TROUBLE. RANGING COMPANIES WERE AUTHORIZED TO PROTECT THE SETTLEMENTS AND ONE OF THE MOST FAMOUS WAS LED BY A YOUNG TENNESSEAN, JOHN COFFEE "JACK" HAYS.

THE ONLY REAL WAY TO FIGHT THE INDIANS WAS FROM HORSEBACK, BUT WHEN IT CAME TO MOUNTED WARFARE, NO ONE WAS SUPERIOR TO THE WILD COMANCHES.

THE TEXANS' MUZZLE LOADERS WERE CLUMSY AFFAIRS AND COULDN'T BE FIRED EFFECTIVELY OR RELOADED AT A GALLOP.

THIS MEANT THE RANGERS HAD TO DISMOUNT AND FIRE ONE VOLLEY, AFTER WHICH THE CIRCLING INDIANS SWOOPED IN TO ATTACK WHILE THE TEXANS WERE DESPERATELY TRYING TO RELOAD.

AS LONG AS THIS SITUATION EXISTED, THE RANGERS WERE COMPELLED TO WAGE A STRICTLY DEFENSIVE WAR AND COULDN'T DO MUCH DAMAGE TO THE HARD-RIDING COMANCHES.

All this changed in 1839 when a youthful Swedish trader named Svante M. Swenson carried back to Texas with him a dozen new-fangled pistols obtained from the New York agent of a young inventor named Samuel Colt.

That same year another Colt booster visited the Republic of Texas, this one with friends in high places. He was John Fuller, an old acquaintance of the Republic's new militaristic poet-president, Mirabeau B. Lamar.

Fuller showed the 5-shooters to President Lamar, hoping to drum up a little business for the starving inventor.

Lamar sent Hays two of the revolvers as a gift and the intrepid ranger was quick to see their merits.

BUT CAPTAIN HAYS WAS TO BE FRUSTRATED IN HIS ATTEMPT TO GET COLTS FOR HIS RANGERS. THE FIRST ORDER OF 180 PISTOLS WENT TO LAMAR'S BRASH NEW NAVY AND HAYS' ONLY SUPPLY WAS THROUGH PRIVATE MERCHANTS LIKE SWENSON.

SOME UNITS OF THE REGULAR ARMY WERE ALSO EQUIPPED WITH THE PATERSON COLT, OR "TEXAS MODEL". THESE ESTEEMED WEAPONS WERE ALWAYS DESTROYED BEFORE ALLOWING THE ENEMY TO CAPTURE THEM.

Then Sam Houston became president for the second time. With Lamar's wild expansionistic schemes put to rest, the needs of Hays' frontier Rangers were finally recognized.

On New Year's Day, 1844, Houston met with Jack Hays and released to him 227 pistols, formerly used by the Navy.

THAT SPRING HAYS GOT HIS CHANCE. IN THE PEDERNALES HILLS HE ASTOUNDED A COMANCHE WARPARTY, LONG ACCUSTOMED TO A FOE WITH ONLY ONE ROUND OF FIREPOWER.

HIT THEM BEFORE THEY CAN RELOAD. NOW!!

THIS BATTLE MARKED A TURNING POINT IN INDIAN WARFARE ON THE FRONTIER. FOR THE FIRST TIME THE TEXANS HELD THE ADVANTAGE IN A RUNNING FIGHT.

THROW DOWN YOUR RIFLES AND MOUNT UP!

BEFORE LONG, THE COMANCHES CAME TO FEAR THE MEN "WITH A SHOT FOR EACH FINGER" AND THEIR POWER BEGAN TO STEADILY DECLINE.

KEEP ON PUSHING 'UM BOYS. DON'T LET UP!

Despite its advantages the Paterson Colt had some problems. It had to be broken down into three parts to be reloaded and was too light to be used as a club.

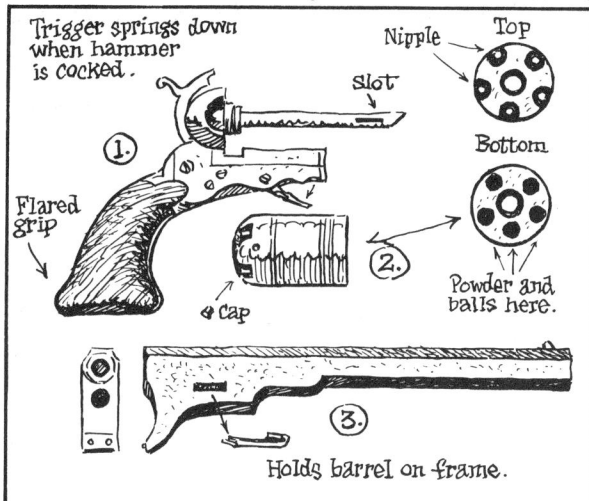

Trigger springs down when hammer is cocked.

Nipple

Top

Slot

①

Flared grip

Cap

②

Bottom

Powder and balls here.

③

Holds barrel on frame.

So Hays and another young Ranger, Samuel Walker, worked on some improvements to make the weapon more suited to the needs of mounted fighting men.

A hinged loading lever under the barrel..

.. and HEAVIER, so's we can club 'um with it!

When the Mexican War commenced, the Rangers signed on as a special regiment of mounted volunteers. They served General Taylor's army as scouts, skirmishers, and couriers, carrying their Colts with them.

After the surrender of Monterrey, Walker went to see Colt in New York with a whittled model of what the Rangers wanted, based on their own experience.

TELL HIM TO MAKE IT HEAVIER SO WE CAN USE IT FOR A CLUB WHEN WE RUN OUT OF BULLETS.

Colt's 5-shooter had met with little success, apart from its popularity in Texas. He was bankrupt and had difficulty even locating one of his No. 5 prototypes.

CAPTAIN WALKER, YOU'RE ON TO SOMETHING HERE...

.. BUT SELLING THE MILITARY BRASS ON IT IS ANOTHER MATTER ENTIRELY.

NEVERTHELESS, THE 32 YEAR OLD INVENTOR ENTHUSIASTICALLY SET ABOUT TO PRODUCE A REVISED VERSION AND FILL THE ORDER FOR A THOUSAND PISTOLS THAT WALKER HAD BROUGHT FROM TEXAS.

BACK IN BUSINESS AT LAST!

What he came up with was an awesome weapon — six shots instead of five, .44 instead of .36 caliber, a lever which permitted reloading without tearing down the gun, a trigger guard, and a hefty weight of 4½ pounds.

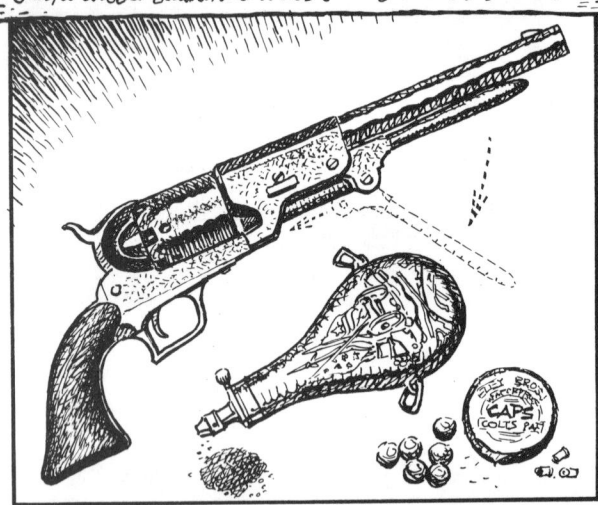

He named it the **WALKER COLT**, in honor of the dashing young war hero who had helped him improve his design— and convince the U.S. Army to buy it!

DON'T WORRY, I'LL SEE TO IT THAT YOU GET YOUR PISTOLS.

THANKS, MR. PRESIDENT.

BY THE TIME THESE PISTOLS WERE DELIVERED, THE THEATRE OF WAR HAD MOVED TO VERA CRUZ. ALL THE TEXAN VOLUNTEERS UNDER COL. HAYS WERE EQUIPPED WITH TWO OF THE NEW 6-SHOOTERS.

DON'T LOSE THEM!! THE ARMY'S SLOW ABOUT REPLACEMENTS..

LOOKIT TH' SIZE OF THEM BEAUTIES!

COLT'S

THEY PROVED THEIR WORTH IN THE HANDS OF "LOS DIABLOS TEJANOS" AND CAPT. WALKER WAS ARMED WITH A SPECIAL PRESENTATION BRACE WHEN HE FELL IN THE STORMING OF HUAMANTLA, OCT. 9, 1847.

SEVERAL LATER MODELS, THE NAVY COLT AND THE COLT DRAGOON, HAD CYLINDER ENGRAVINGS COMMEMORATING EXPLOITS OF THE TEXAS NAVY AND THE BRAVE RANGERS.

Thus the 6-shooter went on to take its place in the winning of the West. Samuel Colt never forgot the Texans for their help in proving his firearm. He wrote: "Texas has done more for me and my armes than all the country..."

jaxon · 83

·91·

END

PROLOGUE: EARLY MORNING IN A DENVER SALOON FINDS TWO CITIZENS SERIOUSLY HUNG OVER.

SAY, HOW'D YOU BOYS LIKE TO KILL A FEW INJUNS?

WHAT'S TH' MATTER? DIDN'T YOU SEE THOSE BODIES WE BROUGHT IN YESTERDAY? INNOCENT WOMEN AND CHILDREN, BUTCHERED LIKE THAT? DON'T IT MAKE YOU FEEL LIKE DOING SOMETHING ABOUT IT?!

I SAW 'EM... HORRIBLE...

MURDERIN' REDSKINS··

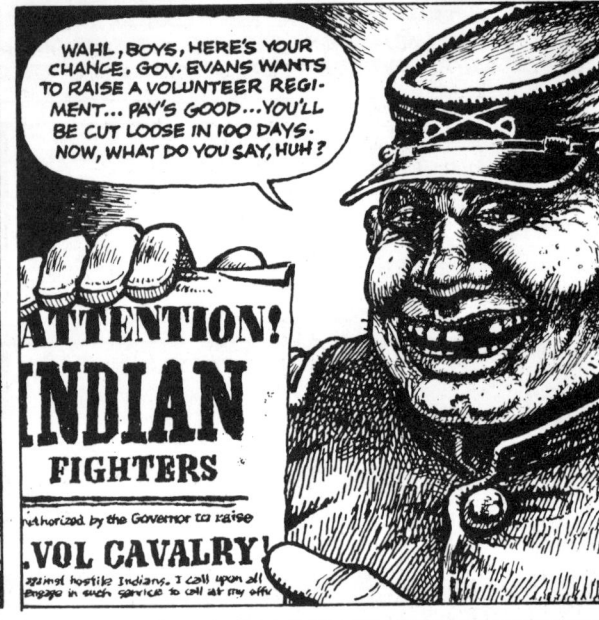

WAHL, BOYS, HERE'S YOUR CHANCE. GOV. EVANS WANTS TO RAISE A VOLUNTEER REGI- MENT... PAY'S GOOD... YOU'LL BE CUT LOOSE IN 100 DAYS. NOW, WHAT DO YOU SAY, HUH?

ATTENTION!
INDIAN
FIGHTERS
authorized by the Governor to raise
.VOL CAVALRY!
against hostile Indians. I call upon all
engage in such service to call at my offi

..AND..WE GIT TO DIVY UP TH' LOOT!! EH? HORSES, MULES, PELTS, EH? AND I HEAR SOME OF THEM CHEYENNE WIMMEN JEST LOVES WHITE STUFF..HOW'BOUT THAT?

EVER HAD ANY OF THET INJUN PUSSY, HUH? HAW HAW

THEY CRAVE IT ALL TH' TIME, I HEAR··SNICKER

YOU BETCHA! CORPORAL, SHOW THESE GENTS WHERE TO SIGN... BARTENDER, A DRINK FOR COLORADO'S FINEST!!

HYUK

'NITS MAKE LICE'

IT'S COLD AND BLEAK ON THE PLAINS THIS NOVEMBER OF 1864 AS THE 3rd REG. OF COLORADO VOLUNTEERS MAKES ITS WAY TO SNOWBOUND FT. LYON.

jaxon.75

SO COLD THAT SLUG AFTER SLUG OF CHEAP WHISKEY FAILS TO WARM THEIR INNARDS.

YES IT'S **COLD**, BUT NOT COLD ENOUGH TO FREEZE THE AMBITIONS OF THE BEAR-LIKE EX-METHODIST PREACHER THAT LEADS THIS MOTLEY CREW, BECAUSE TIME IS RUNNING OUT FOR COL. J.M. **CHIVINGTON**, AND HE IS NOT A MAN TO LET OPPORTUNITY SLIP BY.

CHIVINGTON! THE MAN WHO, DISDAINING A "PRAYING COMMISSION", BLOCKED THE WAY TO THE REBS IN NEW MEXICO AND RETURNED TO DENVER A CONQUERING HERO.

A MAN WHO WILL STOP AT NOTHING TO BOLSTER HIS FALLING POLITICAL STOCK, AND AS EVERYBODY IN THE COLORADO TERRITORY KNOWS, THERE'S NO WAY TO DO THAT LIKE **KILLING INDIANS.**

YESSIR. I SENT SMITH DOWN TO TRADE WITH THEM JUST YESTERDAY. THEY DON'T SUSPECT A THING..

I GOT HERE AS SOON AS I COULD MAJOR. ARE THEY STILL CAMPED DOWN ON SAND CREEK?

GOOD.. I WANT A GUARD POSTED AROUND THIS FORT IMMEDIATELY. NO ONE LEAVES, ON PENALTY OF DEATH— NO ONE — IS THAT UNDERSTOOD?

NOW MEN, MAJOR ANTHONY HERE AND I HAVE GOT A PLAN TO CRUSH THESE BACK-STABBING SAVAGES AND TEACH THEM A LESSON THEY WON'T FORGET... BUT WE'VE GOT TO KEEP A TIGHT LID ON THIS WHOLE OPERATION. THE HOSTILES MUST SUSPECT NOTHING, NOT EVEN OUR BEING HERE.

BEGGING YOUR PARDON, SIR, BUT THE CHEYENNES DOWN ON SAND CREEK AREN'T HOSTILE. IN FACT, MAJ. WYNKOOP HAS GUARANTEED THEIR SAFETY. YOU CAN'T SERIOUSLY BE PLANNING TO ATTACK..

WHO THE HELL IS THIS MAN, MAJOR

CAPT. SOULE, SIR.. ONE OF WYNKOOP'S STAFF OFFICERS..

WELL, CAPT. SOULE, SOME OF US FEEL THAT WYNKOOP DAMN' NEAR LET THE INDIANS RUN THIS FORT AND THAT'S WHY HE'S BEEN RELIEVED. NOW I'VE JUST ABOUT HAD A BELLYFUL OF THE U.S. ARMY PROTECTIN' THESE MURDERERS!

BUT SIR, BLACK KETTLE'S PEOPLE ARE AT PEACE. THEY'RE HERE IN VOLUNTARY COMPLIANCE WITH—

PEACE !?! WHOEVER HEARD OF PEACE-FUL INDIANS, HUH? THEY'RE PEACEFUL WHEN IT SUITS THEM AND THEN THEY SNEAK OUT TO MURDER, BURN AND PILLAGE THE UNPROTECTED CITIZENS OF THIS TERRITORY !!

I SAY DAMN ANY MAN WHO SYMPATHIZES WITH INDIANS!! I'VE COME HERE TO *KILL* INDIANS, AND BY GOD, THAT'S WHAT I'M GONNA' DO! AND YOU'LL DO THE SAME, OR FACE A COURT MARTIAL! *YOU ARE DISMISSED*, CAPT. SOULE!

MY GOD.. HE'S NUTS..

..AND CAPTAIN... PERSONALLY, I WISH YOU *WOULD* BUCK ME, BECAUSE AS FAR AS I'M CONCERNED, THERE'S NO ROOM IN THE U.S. SERVICE FOR YOUR KIND, ANYWAY!

MAJOR, THAT MAN HAS A DEMORALIZED ATTITUDE. I SUGGEST WE KEEP A CLOSE EYE ON HIM..

I ASSURE YOU, SIR, MOST OF THE MEN DON'T FEEL THAT WAY— THEY'RE SPOILING FOR A FIGHT!

GOOD! GOOD! THAT'S WHAT WE'RE HERE FOR! I'VE GOT 600 MEN WITH ME AND THEIR ENLISTMENTS ARE UP REAL SOON. TILL NOW, WE'RE THE LAUGHING STOCK OF THE TERRITORY— THE "BLOODLESS 3rd" THEY CALL US. WELL, NOT ANY MORE! WE'RE GONNA START WADING IN GORE, RIGHT MAJOR?

WE'VE GOT 'EM IN OUR FIST, COL. ALL WE HAVE TO DO IS *SQUEEZE*

A TOTAL VICTORY, THAT'S WHAT WE NEED! *HEADLINE MATERIAL!* AHEM.. AS YOU MAY KNOW MAJOR, GOV. EVANS HAS TAPPED ME TO REPRESENT THE TERRITORY IN THE CAPACITY OF *CONGRESSMAN.* NOW WE'VE ALREADY GOT THE MINERS AND STOCKMEN BEHIND US. STATEHOOD CAN'T BE FAR AWAY.. A WAGONLOAD OF SCALPS WOULD JUST ABOUT CINCH IT AT ELECTION TIME.

THAT'S WONDERFUL, SIR— JUST WONDERFUL! COLORADO NEEDS YOUR TYPE OF LEADERSHIP.

ANTHONY, YOU'RE A GOOD MAN. I HAVE GREAT CONFIDENCE IN YOU— THAT'S WHY I GAVE YOU THIS POST..

WHY THANK YOU, SIR. REST ASSURED I'LL DO MY BEST TO JUSTIFY YOUR EXPECTATIONS...

UNDER COVER OF DARKNESS, CHIVINGTON ORDERS THE TROOPS TO MOVE OUT.

AS THE GREY WINTER DAWN BREAKS OVER SAND CREEK, THE CHEYENNES REST SNUGLY IN THEIR ROBES, CONFIDENT OF THEIR ABSOLUTE SAFETY.

HOOVES DRUMMING ON THE SAND FLATS WAS THE ONLY WARNING OF SOMETHING AMISS...

MY HUSBAND.. AWAKE. A NOISE, LIKE MANY BUF—

SOLDIERS!

AS THE ALARM GOES OUT, BRAVES STUMBLE, HALF-DRESSED, FROM THEIR WARM BEDS..

BLUECOATS! MANY SOLDIERS, COMING INTO CAMP!

THE TRADER, GREY BLANKET SMITH, AND HIS MILITARY ESCORT FROM FT. LYON ARE AS ASTOUNDED AS THE INDIANS AT THE SIGHT THAT GREETS THEIR SLEEP-BEFUDDLED EYES.

SOLDIERS? HERE?? WHAT COULD THEY WANT? I'LL GO TALK TO THEM..

OH IT'S YOU, MAJ. ANTHONY.. WHAT BRINGS YOU FELLOWS OUT SO EARLY?

IT'S SMITH.. SHOOT THE DAMN' OLD SON OF A BITCH! HE'S NO BETTER THAN AN INDIAN!

REALIZING THE TROOPERS' DEADLY INTENT, SMITH AND PVT. LOUDERBACK TURN AND BOLT FOR THEIR TENT.

BAM BLAM

HAW! LOOK AT HIM RUN! ALRIGHT MEN, YOU KNOW WHAT TO DO!!

THE SOLDIERS CHARGE AND THE CHEYENNES SCATTER, LIKE A COVEY OF FRIGHTENED QUAIL.

BLACK KETTLE, ALARMED BUT STILL TRUSTING, TRIES TO CALM HIS PEOPLE AND GATHER THEM TOGETHER...

CHEYENNES!! DO NOT BE AFRAID! THE SOLDIERS WILL NOT HURT YOU!

..UNDER HIS HUGE AMERICAN FLAG, A GIFT FROM GREAT FATHER LINCOLN.

WE HAVE BEEN GIVEN THIS FLAG FOR PROTECTION.. MY PEOPLE, COME! STAND WITH ME.

AS BULLETS GOUGE INTO THE HUDDLED MASS AROUND BLACK KETTLE'S LODGE, WHITE ANTELOPE SINGS HIS DEATH SONG..

WAIT! WAIT! THIS IS A MISTAKE!!

NOTHING LIVES LONG. ONLY THE EARTH—

..UNTIL A SHOT ENDS HIS LIFE.

AND THE MOUNTAINS..

SPLAT!

..HEH HEH EASY AS TAKIN' CANDY FROM A BABY...

THEN THE CARNAGE BEGINS...

..AND LASTS...

..WITHOUT SYMPATHY FOR THE MAIMED...

..OR THE MUTILATED.

WITHOUT MERCY FOR THE DEAD...

BOYS, I'M AGONNA' MAKE ME A TOBACCO POUCH OUTTA OLD WHITE ANTELOPE'S GO-NADS!

..MUCH LESS THE LIVING.

ME NEXT

NOW DON'T BE A HAWG, ELWOOD. SAVE US SOME.

UNTIL THEY HAVE SERVED THEIR CRUEL PURPOSE...

..AND RENDERED UP GRISLY MEMENTOS TO THE VALOR OF THE THIRD COLORADO VOLUNTEERS.

GOT ME A TIT SATCHEL

HOW ABOUT THIS!? FUZZY ONE, HUH?

SOME SOLDIERS, LIKE CAPT. SOULE, POWERLESS TO STOP THE BUTCHERY, WANDER ABOUT IN A DAZE...

MY GOD.. THEY'RE JUST WOMEN & KIDS...

..UNABLE TO BELIEVE THE INHUMANITY THAT ASSAULTS THEIR SENSES.

GAG

SAD DAY THIS, WARRIORS OF THE CHEYENNE, FOR YOU TO BE AWAY, HUNTING THE BUFFALO..

.. AS THE SCALPING KNIVES REAP THEIR GRIM HARVEST AMONG YOUR ELDERS, YOUR WOMEN, YOUR CHILDREN...

POP

.. AS YOUR PONY HERDS ARE ROUNDED UP TO SERVE NEW MASTERS ...

.. AS YOUR ROBES, PELTS AND OTHER THINGS OF VALUE TO THE WHITEMAN ARE PILED HIGH BY GREEDY HANDS..

.. AND THE REST CONSIGNED TO FLAMES.

EXULTING IN THE GORE, J.M. CHIVINGTON SPINS POLITICAL DREAMS, ALREADY IN HIS MIND RECEIVING THE ACCOLADES OF A GRATEFUL CONSTITUENCY BACK IN DENVER.

CONGRESSMAN, HELL, THIS COULD MAKE ME GOVERNOR!

EXCUSE ME, SIR, BUT COMPANY C JUST BROUGHT IN A BATCH OF PRISONERS —

PRISONERS ???! DON'T BOTHER ME WITH CRAP, SGT. WE'RE NOT TAKING PRISON-ERS — BIG OR LITTLE. DON'T YOU KNOW THAT NITS MAKE LICE?

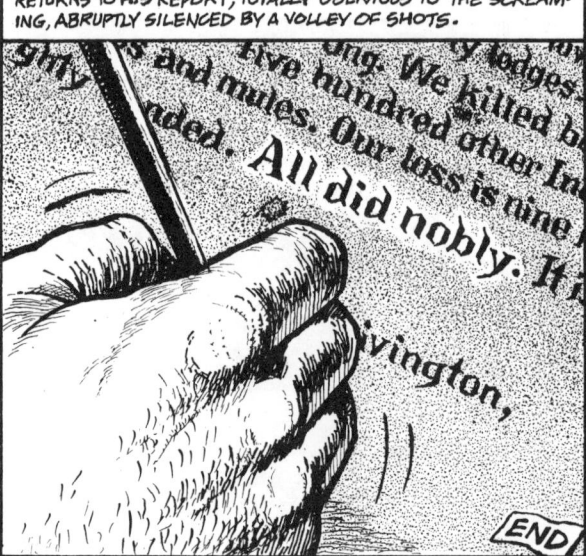

VAGUELY ANNOYED AT THE STUPIDITY OF SERGEANTS, CHIVINGTON RETURNS TO HIS REPORT, TOTALLY OBLIVIOUS TO THE SCREAM-ING, ABRUPTLY SILENCED BY A VOLLEY OF SHOTS.

END

Part II.

jaxon·78

~modern times~

A LONE HIPPIE SCUTTLES ALONG THE DARK STREETS AS UNOBTRUSIVELY AS POSSIBLE.

WHY IS HE SCUTTLING, HIS EYES GLUED TO THE PAVEMENT IN FRONT OF HIM ??

BECAUSE HE'S A WHITE BOY AND HE'S PASSING THROUGH THE DREADED FILLMORE DISTRICT AT NIGHT!

NERVOUSLY HE FUMBLES WITH HIS KEYS AS THE CIRCLE TIGHTENS AROUND HIM.

EVADING THE HORDE OF MERCENARY BANSHEES, YOUNG FRED TODD RIDES THE FREIGHT ELEVATOR UPWARD INTO THE PITCH-BLACK VOID.

IT MIRACULOUSLY LABORS TO A HALT ON THE 3RD FLOOR AND FRED PICKS HIS WAY THROUGH A MINEFIELD OF COUNTERCULTURAL ACTIVITY.

WAY DOWN ON THE END, PAST THE NUDE DANCING TROUPE, THE LIGHTSHOW SETUP, THE IMPROVISED BANDSTAND, AND ASSORTED WORKSHOP/LIVING SPACE, IS A PARTITIONED CORNER.

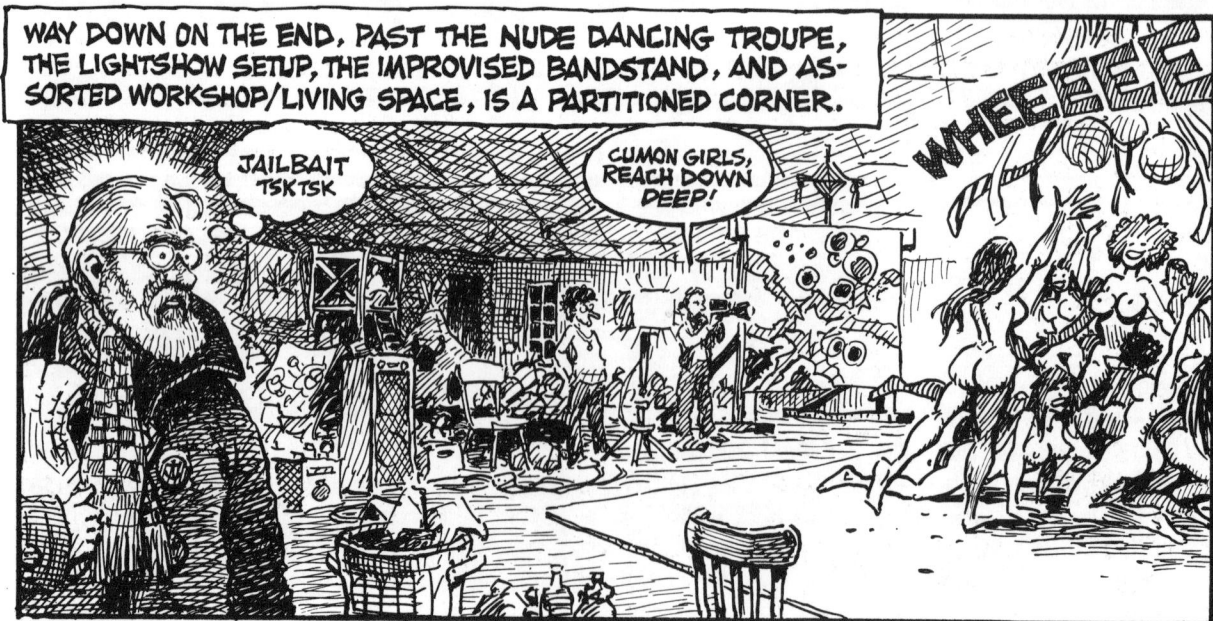

INSIDE ARE TWO PRINTING PRESSES — HOME OF APEX NOVELTIES AND RIP OFF PRESS.

FRED'S BACK WITH TH' BEER!

YEA!!

WHAT TOOK SO LONG? WE'D GIVEN YOU UP FOR DEAD!

OH MAN, JEEZ, YOU WOULDN'T BELIEVE THE SCENE OUT THERE! MOON'S ON TH' CUSP OF SCORPIO!

CHUG CHUGA CHU

IT'S EASY TO TELL WHICH PRESS BELONGS TO THE RIP OFF CREW...

ARRGH.. THERE IT GOES AGAIN!

CUT IT OFF!! QUICK!

MANGLE

RIPPP

SHRED

CONSISTING OF TODD, GILBERT SHELTON, DAVE MORIATY AND ME — JACK JACKSON — EXPATRIATE TEXANS, ALL TRYING TO AVOID ANYTHING THAT VAGUELY RESEMBLES WORK.

LOOK AT THIS MESS!

YEAH.. SOME BODY'S GOTTA CLEAN IT UP.

UH-HUH. SURE DO.

BEING PERPETUALLY STONED AND TOTALLY WITHOUT PRINTING SKILLS, OUR NAME "RIP OFF PRESS" IS PRETTY CLOSE TO REALITY.

AWW, FUCK IT! LET'S GET HIGH AND WORRY ABOUT IT LATER!

GREAT IDEA!

YEAH. NEVER DO TODAY WHAT YOU CAN PUT OFF TILL TOMORROW

I'LL DRINK TO THAT

BUT AT LEAST WE HAD FUN BACK THEN, BEFORE WE HAD TO BECOME COST-EFFECT- IVE CAPITALISTS TO SURVIVE IN THE DOG- EAT-DOG FUNNY BOOK PUBLISHING BIZ.

LOOK WHAT HAPPENED USING THE BLUE PLATE WITH RED INK!

WOW!

FAR OUT!

NOW LET'S TRY A PURPLE-TO- ORANGE SPLIT FOUNTAIN.

KA-CHUNK-KA-CHUNK-A-
NK-KA-CHUNK-KA-CH

WATCHING THE GHETTO SELF-DESTRUCT AROUND US, WE KNEW OUR LOW-RENT DAYS WERE NUMBERED.

GOD ALMIGHTY. THERE'S ANOTHER ONE OVER HERE!

HERE'S SOME MORE FIRE TRUCKS HAULIN' ASS DOWN TURK STREET.

DON'T MATTER. THAT BUILDING'S A GONER...

IN MAY OF 1969 MOWREY'S — WHICH HAD SURVIVED THE EARTHQUAKE AND GREAT FIRE OF 1906 — PERISHED IN ONE OF THOSE RANDOM BLAZES THAT NOBODY EVER KNEW WHO STARTED.

KEEP OUT

AMAZINGLY OUR PRINTING PRESS AND ANTIQUE PAPER CUTTER SURVIVED THE CONFLAGRATION.

WE'LL RISE FROM TH' FLAMES!

I DUNNO', LOOKS SORTA HOPELESS TO ME...

BUT OUR INVENTORY WAS WIPED OUT, AND APEX SHARED THE SAME FATE.

HAW — THEM PERVERTS WUZ DOIN' PORN-NOGRAPHY UP HERE!

GIMME SOME!

ME TOO

SNATCH

JIZ

AFTER THE GREAT FIRE, RIP OFF PRESS WAS SHUFFLED FROM PLACE TO PLACE BY THE SAN FRANCISCO REDEVELOPMENT AGENCY. FIRST WE MOVED IN THE OLD FAMILY DOG OFFICE ON GOUGH ST., THEN A FEW BLOCKS AWAY TO ONE OF THE BUSIEST INTERSECTIONS IN TOWN.

DURING THIS HECTIC PERIOD, ROP CONTINUED DOING COMIX BUT SURVIVED MAINLY ON "COMMERCIAL" PRINT JOBS.

WE FINALLY TIRED OF LIVING WITH THE REDEVELOPMENT AX OVER OUR HEAD...

AND FOUND OURSELVES A SPACIOUS WAREHOUSE AT 17th AND MISSOURI, OUR HOME FOR THE NEXT FIFTEEN YEARS.

WE RENTED OUT THE EXTRA SPACE TO A VARIETY OF ODD-BALL ENTERPRISES. ONE WAS A "NATURAL FOODS" OUTFIT THAT ATTRACTED A PLAGUE OF RODENTS.

DREAMS OF GRANDEUR PROMPTED US TO BUY A HUMONGOUS WEB PRESS — THE KIND THAT HAS TO RUN CONSTANTLY AT PEAK EFFICIENCY OR LOSE MONEY. IT WAS A DISASTER.

THE LEGENDARY *WILD PARTIES* THROWN BY RIP OFF EVOKE FONDER MEMORIES...

UPSTAIRS WAS DEVOTED TO STUDIO SPACE FOR OUR ZANY GROUP OF HARDWORKING ARTISTS.

NOT TO MENTION THE ASPHALT AND TARPAPER ROOF WHERE STAFFERS LOUNGED, RECHARGING THEIR BATTERIES WITH SOLAR ENERGY THE MORNING AFTER...

OH YES — I ALMOST FORGOT THE MAIN REASON FOR ALL THIS MADNESS: A STRING OF TOP-QUALITY UNDERGROUND COMIX THAT KEPT AMERICA LAUGHING THROUGHOUT THE NIXON-REAGAN YEARS. AND THAT WEREN'T EASY FOLKS!

jaxon·88

YOU GOTTA HAVE A LOTTA SOUL...

TO ATTEND A WILLIE NELSON 4th of JULY PICNIC!

EVERYBODY **LOVES** A PICNIC, RIGHT? ESPECIALLY WHEN ITS GOT COLD BEER, B·B·Q, FIREWORKS, MUSIC, AND LOTS OF OTHER NEAT FOLKS GETTIN IT ON TEXAS-STYLE. WELL, HERE'S HOW IT WENT AT THE 3rd ANNUAL BLAST OUT AT LIBERTY HILL...

jaxon 75

GREAT MOMENTS IN AUSTIN MUSIC AT HOUSTON PRICES:
R&B STAR PUTS IT TO HIS LOYAL FANS AT $10 A WHACK

HANDY GUIDE FOR
OUT-OF-STATERS ~ IF YOU'RE ONE OF THOSE COUNTLESS RECENT ARRIVALS TO THE ROMANTIC LONE STAR STATE, DOUBTLESS YOU'LL WANT TO VIEW THE GLAMOROUS COSMIC COWBOY CLOSE UP IN HIS NATIVE HABITAT. BEWARE! YOU COULD MAKE THE FATAL SOCIAL BLUNDER OF MISTAKING THIS NEW, RELATIVELY HARMLESS SUB-SPECIES FOR THE REAL THING ~ THE GENUINE BAD-ASS REDNECK TEXAS COWPOKE! THIS COULD LEAD TO SERIOUS CONSEQUENCES FOR YOUR TENDER EGO ~ LIKE A SWIFT KICK IN THE BUTT! SO, TO EASE YOUR CRITICAL TRANSITION FROM THE CROWDED, VIOLENT, SMOG-RIDDEN EASTERN CITIES TO THE PURE, WIDE-OPEN SPACES, WE PROUDLY PRESENT, FOR THE FIRST TIME EVER, A LONG OVERDUE SURVIVAL MANUAL ON HOW TO IDENTIFY THE MUCH-PUBLICIZED BUT STILL MYSTERIOUS

COZMIC COWBOY!

1. HAT
7. HAIR — ?
CHAW OF BEECH-NUT
EARRING — OPTIONAL
3. SHIRTS
5. JEWELRY
6. T-SHIRT
RED BANDANA
4. PANTS
2. BOOTS

jaxon~ 76

FIRST, APPAREL & ACCESSORIES:

1. **HATS** ~ THIS IS A TOUGHIE, CAUSE **ALL** COWBOYS WEAR HATS, EVEN WHEN THEY BATHE! SWEAT AND GRIME-STAINED, FUNKY STRAW HATS ARE THE TRADEMARK OF THE TRUE COWBOY. HIGH ROLLER FELT OR FUZZY JOBS WITH FEATHER BOAS OR RATTLESNAKE BANDS MEAN HE'S COSMIC.

2. **BOOTS** ~ SCUFFED, CRACKED ACMES USUALLY BELONG TO THE REAL THING. LIZARD, RHINO, HIPPO, OR SNAKE SKIN VARIETIES POINT TO COSMIC TYPES. PLATFORM COWBOY BOOTS ARE A DEAD GIVEAWAY.

3. **SHIRTS** ~ SOLID COLORS OR LOW-KEY PATTERNS WITH PEARL SNAPS ARE THE FAVORITE OF THE WORKING CATTLEMAN. COSMIC COWBOYS LIKE LOUD COLORS, OUT-RAGEOUS PATTERNS — SOME EVEN **WITHOUT POCKETS!** NO REAL COWBOY WOULD EVER BUY A SHIRT WITHOUT POCKETS. THEY MAY BE DUMB, BUT THEY AIN'T STUPID.

4. **PANTS** ~ PANTS INSIDE OF BOOTS, ANOTHER DEAD GIVEAWAY. COSMIC TYPES ARE MUCH TOO FASTIDIOUS FOR THAT SORT OF THING. ALSO CHECK FOR BELLS, BEADS, LEATHER FRINGE OR EMBROIDERED PATCHES. ANY SELF-RESPECTING COWBOY WOULD THROW AWAY RAGGEDY-ASSED JEANS AND BUY NEW ONES.

5. **JEWELRY** ~ TIMEPIECES: REAL COW-PUNCHERS WEAR THE BIG, ROUND JOBS, ATTACHED TO THEIR PANTS BY A CHAIN. IF THEY'RE PROGRESSIVE, THEY MIGHT HAVE A BULOVA OR AN ELGIN WRISTWATCH. COSMIC COWBOYS, ON THE OTHER HAND, HAVE ELABORATE, FOREIGN, COMPUTORIZED, NEVER-WIND-DOWN JOBS ~ SET AMIDST GAUDY TURQUOISE OR OTHER AUSTINTATIOUS STUFF.
THEY'RE ALSO FOND OF WEARING NECKLACES ~ PUKA SHELL, HEISHI BEADS, COKE SPOONS, AND PONDEROUS SQUASH BLOSSOM AFFAIRS ~ AS WELL AS COVERING THEIR FINGERS WITH RINGS OF ALL SHAPES, SIZES, AND DEGREES OF BAD TASTE. REAL COWBOYS KEEP IT PRETTY BASIC ~ BELT BUCKLE AND WEDDING BAND.

6. **T-SHIRTS** ~ IF YOU'RE STILL HAVING TROUBLE DE-CIDING, ASK TO SEE HIS T-SHIRT. IF IT'S AN ESOTERIC OR PSYCHEDELIC NUMBER, YOU'RE OKAY. IF IT'S NOT, SLOWLY PICK YOURSELF UP AND BACK OFF. HE'S GOT YOU FIGURED FOR A FAG. UNLESS YOU'RE A GIRL...

7. **HAIR** ~ IF ALL ELSE FAILS, OBSERVE LENGTH OF HAIR... TRUE COWBOYS HAVEN'T LEARNED ABOUT SHAMPOO YET, SO THEY KEEP IT SHORT TO COPE WITH DIRT, GREASE AND SWEAT ~ THINGS COSMIC COWBOYS RARELY COME IN CONTACT WITH.

HABITS: IF YOU CAN'T SPOT A COSMIC COWBOY FROM THE WAY HE LOOKS, SOMETIMES HIS HABITS AND LIFESTYLE WILL HELP OUT. FOR INSTANCE, HIS **TRUCK**. CLOSE SCRUTINY IS NECESSARY TO PICK OUT THE SUBTLE CLUES. YOU MAY BE FOOLED AT FIRST. LOOK FOR THINGS LIKE TAPE DECKS, CB UNITS, FAT TIRES, GUN RACKS, FENCE BUILDING EQUIPMENT, AND BALES OF HAY.

CHECK OUT THEIR **BARS**: COSMIC COWBOYS LIKE BARS WITH HANGING PLANTS, ARMADILLO ART, AND STAINED GLASS, SALVAGED FROM DEMOLISHED TEXAS HISTORICAL LANDMARKS.

REAL COWBOYS DON'T GIVE A SHIT, LONG AS THE BEER'S COLD.

THE BIG THING, OF COURSE, IS THE MUSIC SCENE. IT'S HERE THAT COSMIC COWBOYS REIGN SUPREME. THEY'RE ON SOLID GROUND NOW FOR SURE, NO DOUBT ABOUT IT. **EVERYBODY** LOVES 'EM — NASHVILLE FAWNS OVER THEM, THE MASS MEDIA DESCENDS, CULT FIGURES ARE ENSHRINED, A SENSE OF **DESTINY**, OF **SACRED PURPOSE** IS SPAWNED — WHAT DOES IT ALL **MEAN** ???

MEANWHILE, THE TRUE COWBOY TAKES HIS MUSIC WHERE HE CAN GET IT ~ NOT TOO AVANT-GARDE, BUT SOULFUL AS HELL. HE'S STILL GLIDING SOMEWHERE OVER THOSE FUNKY TEXAS DANCEHALL SAWDUST FLOORS, OBLIVIOUS TO THE RISING AND FALLING STARS ON THE PAGES OF BILLBOARD. AFTER ALL, YOU CAN SEE THE *REAL* **THING** MOST ANY NIGHT IN THAT **BIG** TEXAS SKY.

YOUR CHEATIN' HEART..

YOU AIN'T GOT **NO** MANNERS A'TALL..

EEEKK

THEIR WOMEN: TEXAS WOMEN ARE TEXAS GOLD, ANY WAY YOU SLICE IT. YANKEE LADIES HAVE POSSIBILITIES TOO, WITH A LITTLE LEARNING ~ BUT THERE'S THOUSANDS OF THEM, AND SO LITTLE TIME.

HEY BABY, WANNA GO TAKE SOME QUAAS AND **GET DOWN.**

WHAT A STUD!

REAL COWBOYS USUALLY WIND UP MARRYING GIRLS THEY'VE KNOWN ALL THEIR LIFE. MIGHT AS WELL, CAUSE YOU CAN'T SHACK-UP IN THE BOONDOCKS WITHOUT THE WHOLE COUNTY KNOWING ANYWAY.

THERE'S A BIG GOAT-ROPIN' OVER AT LEANDER NEXT WEEK, IF YOU'RE INTERESTED...

WHAT A **STUD...**

DRINKING: NO HELP HERE, THEY BOTH DRINK GOD-AWFUL AMOUNTS OF BEER. A CLOSER LOOK, HOWEVER, SOMETIMES REVEALS THE DIFFERENCE.

ASK IF HE'S GOT ANY **ROLL-ING PAPERS.** IF HE HANDS YOU BUGLERS, FORGET IT. MENTHOLATED STRAWBERRY AMERICAN FLAG BICENTENNIAL PAPERS ARE A SAFE BET.

TAKE YOUR PICK..

CONSCIOUSNESS EXPANDERS: REAL COWBOYS WILL OFFER YOU A CHAW OF BEECH-NUT. COSMIC COWBOYS PREFER REEFERS OR, IF YOU'RE LUCKY, COCAINE AND QUAALUDES.

READING MATERIAL: THIS IS A REALLY TOUGH ONE, CAUSE **NEITHER** KIND OF COWBOY CAN **READ.** HOWEVER, REAL COWBOYS LIKE TO **LOOK** AT THE **PICTURES** IN FARM AND RANCH JOURNAL... WHEREAS COSMIC COWBOYS PREFER THOSE IN THE ROLLING STONE....

HE LOOKS AT ROLLING STONE BECAUSE HE WANTS TO SEE HIS PICTURE THERE. BUT MOSTLY, HE WANTS OTHER PEOPLE TO SEE HIS PICTURE THERE.

OH WELL, MAYBE NEXT ISSUE...

GET DRUNK AND BE SOMEBODY

IF NATIONAL RECOGNITION OF THE TEXAS SCENE FALTERS, WE SHUDDER TO THINK OF THE MEASURES PERMISSIVE COUNTRY MUSICIANS MIGHT ADOPT TO REGAIN THE SPOTLIGHT ~ THINGS LIKE PROGRESSIVE COUNTRY S+M, REDNECK GLITTER ROCK, NEEDLEFREAK TEXAS SWING, C+W SODOMY.

OH BABY, WHY YOU TREAT YO' BARNDOOR MAN SO BAAAAD

BAAAAD

BAAD

THINGS TO AVOID: ONCE YOU ARE ABLE TO IDENTIFY THE GENUINE COWBOY, HERE'S SOME THINGS TO AVOID, CAUSE THEY MIGHT MAKE HIM MAD, AND YOU DON'T WANT TO DO THAT... BELIEVE ME. FIRST, TRY TO SHUCK YOUR FOREIGN ACCENT AS SOON AS POSSIBLE. DON'T SAY "SAN AN·TON·I·O" ~ IT'S SAN ANTONE; LIKEWISE, "MEXICAN" ~ IT'S MESKIN. FAILURE TO MASTER THESE LINGUISTIC NICETIES WILL MAKE YOU STAND OUT LIKE A SORE EYE.

YOUR WIFE A SAN ANTONIO MEXICAN?

WHUD YEW SAY, BOAH??

DON'T TRY TO IMPRESS REAL COWBOYS. THEY'RE NOT EASILY IMPRESSED. SAFER OPENING CONVERSATION DEALS WITH EXISTENTIAL, NITTY-GRITTY MATTERS LIKE THE WEATHER.

NICE HEIFER YOU GOT THERE, PARD. REMINDS ME OF THAT ELTON JOHN LINE... YOU HEARD THAT ONE?

..TURKEY...

BE CAREFUL ABOUT INSULTING REMARKS TO THEIR WOMEN ~ ESPECIALLY WAITRESSES. COWBOYS ARE OVERLY PROTECTIVE OF THIS, THE FINEST EXAMPLE OF TEXAS WOMANHOOD.

WHAT? NO BAGELS?! THEN HOW ABOUT RAVIOLI ON THE SIDE...

NOW THAT ALL YOU VISITIN' FOLKS KNOW THE ROPES, WE'RE SURE YOU'LL WANT TO RUSH RIGHT DOWN AND DECK YOURSELF OUT IN THE PROPER DUDS. HAPPY TRAILS, PODNER.

?

.. I READ ABOUT IT IN THE Sun

jaxon · END

the RISE and RAPID DECLINE of Austin Tacious

WAY BACK IN 1837 THE CAPITAL OF TEXAS WAS A TENT CITY THROWN UP IN A PESTILENCE-RIDDEN BAYOU AREA BY A.C. ALLEN, A CLEVER REAL ESTATE DEVELOPER FRIEND OF SAM HOUSTON'S.

EVERYBODY HATED IT EXCEPT POSSIBLY ALLEN AND THE MAN IT WAS NAMED AFTER...

.. EVEN BUILD YOU BOYS A FINE CAPITOL IF YOU'LL LOCATE HERE, SAM..

WAHL, I HAVE'TA ADMIT, THE TOWN HAS GOT A REAL CATCHY NAME..

WHEN LAMAR BECAME PRESIDENT, HE DIDN'T MUCH CARE TO PRESIDE OVER THE REPUBLIC IN A TOWN NAMED FOR HIS ARCH-ENEMY. HE FOUND A PLACE MORE TO HIS LIKING WHILE HUNTING BUFFALO ON THE COLORADO RIVER, DEEP IN INDIAN TERRITORY.

WHAT DO YOU CALL THIS SCENIC SPOT, FRIEND?

WATERLOO, IF YOU GET WHAT I MEAN..

WATERLOO?? I DON'T GET IT...

NEITHER DO I, BUT THERE'S A NICE LOCATION FOR A HOLIDAY INN!

WHEN SURVEYORS MOVED IN UNDER EDWIN WALLER, THE LOCAL RESIDENTS WERE DISMAYED..

OH GOD— WHITE PEOPLE!! THE NEIGHBORHOOD'S GOING TO HELL!

I KNEW IT WAS TOO GOOD TO LAST..

AN EIGHT FOOT STOCKADE WAS ERECTED AROUND THE NEW CAPITOL BUILDING TO KEEP THE PESKY REDSKINS OUT.

HEY, IS THIS WHERE TH' BIG PICNIC'S AT?

BEAT IT! WILLIE NELSON AIN'T EVEN BEEN BORN YET.

WISH THEY'D STAY OUT ON THEIR SIDE OF TOWN, WHERE THEY BELONG!

BY 1850 THE POPULATION HAD DWINDLED DOWN FROM A RECORD 856 TO A MERE 629 CITIZENS.

WHAT WE NEED IS A BIG SCHOOL TO GET SOME PEOPLE IN HERE..

SAM HOUSTON NEVER CARED MUCH FOR THE PLACE AND KEPT TRYING TO MOVE THE CAPITAL SOMEWHERE ELSE.

NO SALOONS, NO WIMMEN.. GOT TO BE THE WORST PLACE IMAGINABLE FOR RUNNING A NATION..

GOOMBAH MERCANTILE & DRY GOODS

ROSITA'S TAMALE

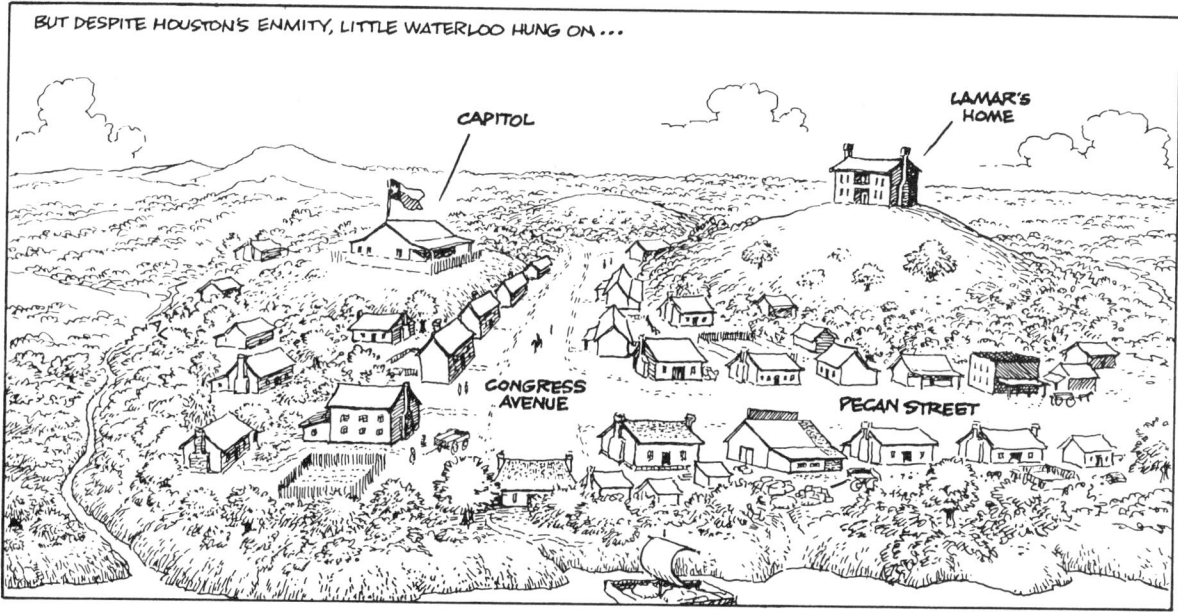

BUT DESPITE HOUSTON'S ENMITY, LITTLE WATERLOO HUNG ON...

CAPITOL

LAMAR'S HOME

CONGRESS AVENUE

PECAN STREET

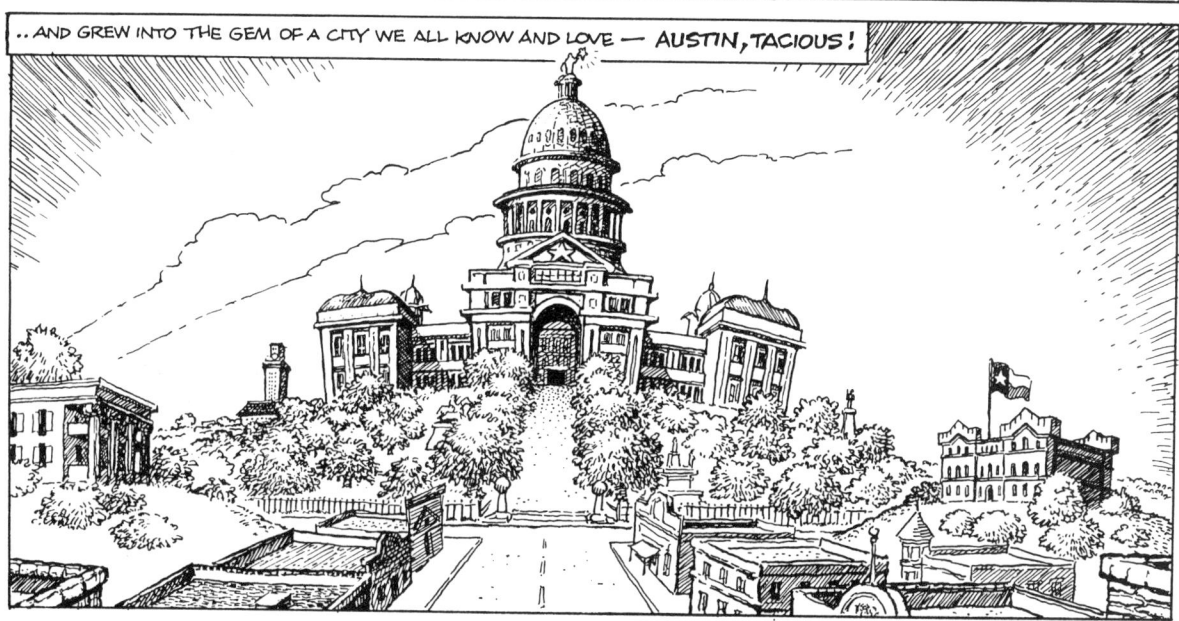

..AND GREW INTO THE GEM OF A CITY WE ALL KNOW AND LOVE — AUSTIN, TACIOUS!

Next: The Beginning of the End.

USED TO BE, APPROACHING AUSTIN FROM ANY DIRECTION, TWO AND ONLY TWO MONUMENTS BROKE THE FLAT SKYLINE— ONE DEDICATED TO EDUCATION AND THE OTHER TO POLITICS.

BUT IN THE MID-SIXTIES THE LITTLE MONSTERS CAME OF AGE AND BEGAN TO EXTEND THEIR GRASPING TENTACLES, UPROOTING AND DESTROYING THE PEACEFUL RESIDENTIAL NEIGHBORHOODS BETWEEN AND TO THE EAST OF THEM.

WHAT HAD ONCE BEEN LOW-COST, FURNISHED HOUSES FOR STUDENTS AND OFFICE WORKERS..

..BECAME ACRES OF PARKING LOTS, AN EMPTY, DESOLATE CHESSBOARD, SET FOR FUTURE POWERPLAYS BY THE SPRAWLING RIVAL BUREAUCRACIES.

THE CONCEPT OF STUDENT HOUSING WAS REDEFINED TO FIT THE PIGEON-HOLE MENTALITY OF OUR NEW SOCIETY.

AND SO, LIKE A LASTING TRIBUTE TO MEDIOCRITY, AUSTIN'S FUTURE GHETTOS SPRING INTO BEING.

Next: The Shit Hits the Fan.

THEN, SLOWLY AT FIRST, AUSTIN'S SKYLINE BEGAN TO **CHANGE.** THE LARGE-BREASTED DOME AND THE PHALLIC TOWER BECOME **LOST** IN A MAZE OF STERILE LINEAR MONUMENTS TO A **THIRD GOD — BUSINESS.** WHAT DARK MYSTERIES THE HIGH PRIESTS OF GREED EXPLORE IN THESE **INSCRUTABLE TEMPLES,** ONLY THE ANCIENT AZTECS MIGHT GUESS.

OH GREAT **SPIRIT** OF **BANK AMERICARD,** OF **MASTER CHARGE,** SECURE US MORE FIXED ASSETS, BRING US MORE EXPRESSWAYS, MORE NEW BUILDING PERMITS BABBLE BABBLE

..STRIKE ZONING ORDINANCES DEAD BY YOUR BENIGN NEGLECT, SEND US MORE ASPHALT AND CONCRETE, GIVE US A SELF-SERVING, "PROGRESS MINDED" CITY COUNCIL... BABBLE BABBLE BA$I...

MONEY

BANK

NOT TO BE OUTDONE BY THE PUSHY UPSTARTS DOWNTOWN, PUSHY POLITICIANS RACE TO **GLORIFY THEMSELVES** WITH PYRAMIDS BUILT BY THE SWEAT OF OPPRESSED TEXAS TAXPAYERS.

FASTER, **FASTER,** YOU CLOWNS! THAT BUILDING'S GOTTA BE FINISHED BY TIME I'M **GOVERNOR!**

LEMME **BITE** 'UM BOB — C'MON, LEMME...

THE RICH FARMLANDS, GRAZING LANDS, AND PICTURESQUE HILL COUNTRY AROUND AUSTIN ARE BEING SWALLOWED UP BY MONEY-HUNGRY DEVELOPERS THAT WOULD CAUSE EVEN HOUSTON'S ENTERPRISING FOUNDER TO BLUSH WITH ENVY.

NOW AIN'T THIS BETTER THAN A EMPTY PASTURE AND A BUNCH OF OL' DUMB **COWS** ??

WAHL, I KINDA MISS TH' WAY IT **WUZ,** BUT YOU CAN'T STOP PROGRESS I GUESSS...

SLEAZY ACRES PETITE RANCHETTES FOR THE JET SET. *from* $80,000— FLY-BY-NITE, DEVELOPERS **QUICK-N-DIRTY, INC.** CONTRACTORS AND BUILDERS

ROAAR

Next: Austin Tomorrow.

NO PLACE, NO MATTER HOW PRETTY, IS SACRED TO THE REAL ESTATE HUSTLERS — NOT EVEN **BARTON SPRINGS**, ONCE DESCRIBED AS THE MOST BEAUTIFUL NATURAL SPRING IN CENTRAL TEXAS, BUT NOW A CESSPOOL FOR THE TACKY BOXES PERCHED ON ITS RIM. WHAT'S NEXT, A MACDONALD'S ON TOP MT. BONNELL?

OF COURSE, ONCE THE MESS IS IN TH' POT, WE'VE GOT TO HAVE SOME WAY TO **STIR** IT, RIGHT? SMOG AND **POLLUTION** CAN'T BE FAR AWAY FOR OUR CLEAR BLUE SKIES.

WE HEAR A LOT OF NOISE THESE DAYS ABOUT "FUTURE PLANNING" AND "CONTROLLED GROWTH", BUT IS **THIS** REALLY WHAT WE WANT OUR TOWN TO LOOK LIKE?

jaxon·77

The End

SILENT INVASION

In all my years with th' Border Patrol, Clyde, I never seen nothing like it. Crossing the river, one after another.

Why, it's a regular INVASION!

Coming in here, taking our jobs, our housing—destroying our cultural institutions and all.

They don't even speak our language.

Doesn't do no good to try and discourage them. They just keep on a' coming...

At first I felt sorry for the poor devils but ENOUGH IS ENOUGH!

CLYDE

It's like th' President sez: We got to get tough in Texas and re-establish control of our borders.

Even if it means OUTRIGHT WAR!

YOU HAVE JUST CROSSED THE RED RIVER WELCOME TO TEXAS

OH GOD, VIRGIL, HERE COMES ANOTHER LOAD!!

WHAT'S IN THE TRAILER SHORTY?

ALL TH' PROBLEMS THEY WANTED TO LEAVE BEHIND..

CHUG CHUG SPUTTER

U-HAUG

TEXAS BOR BUST

URBAN SPRAWL CRIME UNEMPLOYMENT NUKE SLUMS POLLUTION INDUSTRY MICHIGAN 052491

jaxon·83

WHY DO TEXANS HATE YANKEES SO MUCH?
(LET ME COUNT THE WAYS...)

Some authorities think the defense mechanisms that Texans have had to adapt for survival accounts for the saying that everything here either STICKS, STINGS or STINKS.

Certainly the hostility that Texans nourish for "Yankees" dates back to prehistoric times.

The first humans to arrive (from the NORTH, naturally) felt it...

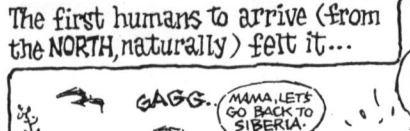

... but since they couldn't beat th' primordial Texans, learned to join 'um.

Animosities were heightened when the savage Comanches visited Texas...

* "Caca-do-wah" translates as "Snowbird," possibly the very first use of this term for uninvited seasonal guests.

...and liked it so much they decided to stay.

While the poor "natives" were nursing bruised heads, the Spanish snuck in the back door.

Like the uppity Comanches, these snobbish Europeans didn't think much of the local talent.

However, the first Spaniards easily adjusted to laid-back Texan ways. Soon they too knew a Yankee on sight.

Or at least they thought they did— until the Real McCoy showed up!

But even these obnoxious, hard-assed types were quickly absorbed and became mellow Texans...

*Author's note: Secret documents from the Papal Archives reveal that "Techas"– from which Texas is derived– really means "Yankee Go Home", not "Friends" as the Spanish missionaries pretended.

...after they had cleaned out the aborigines, of course.

Before long the early arriving whites were also able to detect when a Yankee was in the vicinity.

This subtlety was somewhat lost on the older inhabitants, along with a lot of other things.

Ignoring EONS of prehistory, experts are fond of saying that the anti-Yankee attitudes of most Texans came with the collapse of the Confederacy...

...and the beginning of "Reconstruction", a fancy word for Gang-Banging on a cultural scale.

✳ THIS IS NOT A BLACK SOLDIER. IT IS A WHITE DRAFT DODGER CLEVERLY DISGUISED TO LOOK LIKE A BLACK SOLDIER. ACTUALLY THERE WERE NO NEGROES IN TEXAS DURING RECONSTRUCTION, ALL HAVING MOVED TO DETROIT IN THE BIG HEAT WAVE OF '64.

While being ripped off at home, Texans tried to make a living by trailing cows to northern markets. Granted their reception did little to inspire any great modification of feelings toward Yankees.

But Reconstruction was a drop in the bucket compared to the PRESENT PHASE, shortened to "Construction", altho some prefer Development, Sun Belt Mania, Real Estate Boom, Land Bonanza, etc etc.

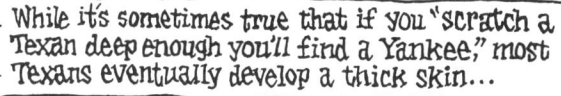

While it's sometimes true that if you "scratch a Texan deep enough you'll find a Yankee," most Texans eventually develop a thick skin...

...always necessary to survival in this neck of the woods...

...but never moreso than now.

jaxon·83

END

SUTHERLY BREEZE

* (STNP — South Texas Nuclear Project)

OAT WILLIE'S MID-LIFE CRISIS

REMEMBER HOW WE USED TO SMUGLY SAY, "WE ARE THE PEOPLE OUR PARENTS WARNED US AGAINST?" WELL, LATELY I'VE FOUND MYSELF SAYING THE SAME THINGS MY PARENTS USED TO SAY TO ME!

TURN THAT RACKET DOWN!!

♪♫ FIGHT FOR YER RIGHT TO PARR-TY ♫♪

WHATEVER HAPPENED TO OUR DREAMS???

PEACE LOVE FREEDOM HUMAN DIGNITY JUSTICE EQUALITY SAFE SEX CHEAP DOPE

ZZZZ

I KNOW!! I'LL CALL GOD NOSE! HE NOSE TH' SCORE..

RING!! RING!!

..CLICK..

WE'RE GLAD YOU PHONED SORRY, GOD'S NOT HOME BUT HE'LL BE BACK BEFORE TOO LONG ♫♪

HE'S ON THE COAST WITH THE HOLY GHOST JUST LEAVE YOUR NAME WITH TH' HEAVEN'LY HOST

WE GIVE A HOOT AS DOES TH' SNOOT SO SPEAK RIGHT UP WHEN YOU HEAR GABE TOOT!

BLAAAAT!!

UH-OH.. I GOT HIS ANSWERING MACHINE..

TAPPITY TAPPITY

TAPPITY TAPPITY TAP

YO, NOSE, IT'S ME, OAT WILLIE.. I WAS HOPING TO REACH YOU BUT—

CLICK

WILLIE! HEY MAN, I'M REALLY HERE... JUST HAD TH' MACHINE ON WHILE I PLAYED SOME *BABBEL* WITH THE GANG.. HEH HEH.. SAY, KNOW ANY WORDS WITH 2 U's, A CUNEIFORM AND A RUNE?

NO??? WELL, WHAT'S UP THESE DAYS? WHAT'RE YOU DOING?

WHAT AM *I* DOING?? THE QUESTION, NOSE, IS WHAT ARE **YOU** DOING! WE'RE IN A LOT OF TROUBLE DOWN HERE... *HUNDREDS* OF PLANT, ANIMAL, AND CULTURAL SPECIES ARE GOING *EXTINCT!!*

"THEY'RE DESTROYING THE WORLD'S RAIN FORESTS TO MAKE PAPER BAGS!"

"THERE'S A *HOLE* IN THE OZONE LAYER DOWN AT TH' SOUTH POLE!!"

WHEW!

EACH YEAR MORE AND MORE PEOPLE GO HUNGRY AND HOMELESS..

JACK JACKSON a.k.a. "Jaxon," was born in Pandora, Texas, on May 15, 1941.

He first rose to fame as an underground cartoonist; some highlights from that period are reprinted in *Optimism of Youth* (Fantagraphics Books). But Jackson soon moved towards historical strips. His earliest ones are discussed in Joseph Witek's scholarly study, *Comic Books As History* (University Press of Mississippi). Apart from *God's Bosom*, some of Jackson's other historically-oriented books include: *Long Shadows*, an illustrated text history of the Indians who stood in the way of European expansion (Paramount Publishing); two volumes of his "Texas trilogy," *Comanche Moon*, the life of Comanche chief Qanah Parker (Rip Off/Last Gasp), and *Los Tejanos*, a biography of Texan independence fighter Juan Seguin (Fantagraphics Books). The third volume, *The Lost Cause*, will focus on the life of Texas badman John Wesley Hardin in Reconstruction times.

Quite different in atmosphere is *The Secret of San Saba*, an X-rated history in the Spanish colonial period, with a heavy dose of fantasy (Kitchen Sink). Other of Jackson's works include his renditions of *The Last of the Mohicans*, the life of Christopher Columbus, and Joe Lansdale's *Dead in the West* (Dark Horse Comics).

In addition to his comic work, Jackson has provided illustrations for a number of "legit" books about Texas history, as well as becoming something of a recognized historian himself. His *Los Mesteños* (Texas A&M Press) was a prize-winning study of Spanish ranching in Texas and contains a slew of illustrations. Early mapping is his latest obsession, and The Book Club of Texas will release Jackson's *Flags Along the Coast* this year in a deluxe, limited edition format. Another study in the series will appear next year as *Shooting the Sun* — projected as two volumes (The Book Club of Texas). Maps, being visual windows into the past, are exciting to an artist-historian like Jackson, but the "comic" medium remains his favorite mode of expression for dealing with history.

His most recent work is *Threadgill's Comics*, which looks at Austin's music scene, focusing on Janis Joplin (who got her start at Threadgill's beer joint).